SUMMARY

I0623893

Eloise Kolby leaves her hometown of Chicago and arrives in 1950s Hollywood with dreams of becoming a movie star. While waiting for her big break, she falls for charming script-writer Ross Wilson. But when Ross promises her a big surprise, it's not a ring, but a new project on location in Italy —for him alone. Putting her dreams on hold, she agrees to investigate a house he inherited in a small desert town outside LA.

Ridgecrest postman Victor Burnham has always wanted to buy the property on Ivy Lane. But from the moment the beautiful, mysterious blonde moves into "his" house, his life becomes complicated. Their daily rendezvous at the mailbox has tongues wagging and Victor longing to share his dream house.

When Eloise's long-awaited letter arrives, signaling Ross's return, she must choose—her new life on Ivy Lane with a steadfast postman and the promise of a family or the allure of fame and Hollywood glamour. Whose heart will be stamped *Return to Sender*?

19 IVY LANE

AUBREY WYNNE

PLATO PUBLISHING

Editing by The Editing Hall

Cover by Taylor Sullivan

CHARMING IN CHICAGO SERIES

Merry Christmas, Henry (Charming in Chicago #1)
  Dante's Gift (Charming in Chicago #2)
  Paper Love (Charming in Chicago #3)
  For the Love of Laura Beth (Charming in Chicago #4)
  19 Ivy Lane (Charming in Chicago #5)

Other Small Town sweet romances
  Saving Grace (A Small Town Romance #1)

Just for Sh*#$ and Giggles short story series
  To Cast A Cliche (A Just for Sh*#$ and Giggles Short Story #1)
  Pete's Mighty Purty Privies (A Just for Sh*#$ and Giggles Short Story #2)

Historical Romance
  Once Upon a Widow series (sweet Regency)
  Paddy's Peelers series(historical mystery)

Subscribe to Aubrey's newsletter for new releases, exclusive excerpts, and free stories:

Newsletter: http://www.subscribepage.com/k3f1z5

PROLOGUE

March 1950
Los Angeles, California

$\mathcal{V}$ictor leaned back in his chair, blowing out a long breath. His father had been reluctant to sleep, too worried about his wife to close his eyes. They had come to Los Angeles hoping to find better news. But the physicians had the same message: Heart attack. Bed rest, take it easy, no stress or extreme physical exertion. He watched Pop's chest rise and fall, the glare of the ceiling lights shining off his bald head, his weathered face slack with exhaustion.

Pop had been a janitor at the high school since before Victor had been born. He had become the head of maintenance for the school district ten years later. While his work didn't include much heavy lifting, Mr. Burnham spent long, hot days in the summer preparing the buildings for the next school year. The school board was concerned he might not be able to continue. There had been an offer to bring in extra help, teenage boys needing a summer job, which Pop had refused out of pride.

"WHAT WILL SHE DO WITHOUT ME?" *The pain in Pop's eyes wrenched Victor's heart. "I don't have enough saved yet to take care of her when I'm gone."*

"Then it looks like you're stuck here for a while longer, Pop." Victor squeezed his father's hand, hoping Mom didn't walk in on this conversation. "The doctor said with proper care you could be around for years to come."

"He also said I could drop dead tomorrow. It was a waste of money to come here." Mr. Burnham swiped a hand over his weathered face. "More money I can't leave for your mother."

"Pop, I'll always take care of Mom." He paused, then added for a bit of comic relief, "If she'll let me. You know how stubborn and independent she can be."

"VICTOR, hun, why don't you grab a bite at that diner around the corner? You need a break." His mother's soft voice roused him. She rubbed his back in little circles as if he were still her little boy. "They have such good blue-plate specials."

He nodded and stood, then stretched. "Yeah, good idea." He stood, towering over the petite five-foot frame, and kissed the top of her auburn head.

Leaving the hospital, the honks and yells of passersby and cab drivers echoing around him, he walked along the crowd toward the corner. He turned left and stopped under the sign *Harvey's Diner.* It was midafternoon, so the place wasn't packed like lunch had been yesterday. He pushed open the door and scanned the red leather booths and speckled tabletops. He decided to take a stool at the counter.

Grabbing a menu, he perused the lunch options. When he

looked up to see the daily specials on the board, he found a beautiful blonde waitress smiling at him with a pot of coffee in her hand.

"What can I get you?" she asked.

Victor blinked, feeling as if he were falling into the depths of those luminous blue eyes.

"Coffee?" she asked. "A Coke?"

He blinked again and read her name tag. *Eloise*. "Uh, yes, coffee. Please," he added, a smile curving his lips. She slipped her order pad back into her apron pocket and flipped over the cup sitting in the saucer before him.

"Are you hungry?"

He nodded. "I was just looking at the specials."

"I'll give you a minute, then."

Victor watched her walk away, the pale-yellow cotton uniform hugging the woman's curves, her mid-length flaxen hair pulled back at the nape of a long, slender neck. His reaction to her surprised him. He wasn't the type of man who felt an attraction to a woman so quickly. Especially a total stranger.

He watched as she took the order of a couple at one of the booths. Her smile was contagious, her movements graceful, her voice a pitch lower than the usual female octave. She had shapely calves, telling him she was active. Maybe she'd been in track or some kind of sport in high school. He guessed her to be about twenty or a little younger.

When she returned, he ordered the meatloaf with mashed potatoes. Eloise made chitchat, asking if he was in LA sightseeing.

"No, my dad's here seeing a heart specialist," Victor replied, sipping at his black coffee.

"Oh, I'm sorry to hear that. I hope it works out okay," she said, reaching out a ringless left hand to give his wrist a squeeze.

Her touch was electric. The warmth sizzled up his arm, and he took a breath. She was gorgeous and kind. A pang of regret poked his gut, wishing he'd met her at a diner in Ridgecrest rather than Los Angeles. He would have asked her out.

"Are you from LA?" he asked.

She laughed. "Oh, no. I came from Chicago. I want to be an actress."

"I bet you could be anything you wanted," he blurted out.

She blushed. "Thank you. I've been here only a few weeks, so cross your fingers for me."

"I will," he said, meaning it.

When Victor returned to the hospital, his mother met him at the door. "Your father's ready to go home."

Behind her, Pop said, "If they can't work any miracles, we might as well get on with life. I want to sleep in my own bed tonight."

CHAPTER 1

August 1950
Los Angeles, California

*E*loise Kolby wiggled her toes in the sand, the cool, tan grains tickling and scratching the bottom of her feet. Frothy waves lapped rhythmically at her ankles, gently pushing the hem of her skirt back and forth against the pebbly beach as if quietly waltzing on its own. She softly hummed "You're Breaking My Heart" and imagined Vic Damone next to her, watching the sun sink into the Pacific Ocean.

She smiled at the sound of children laughing. A mother's reprimand followed, but she soon joined in her children's laughter. It made Eloise think of Chicago and home and her brothers and sisters. Was her father's new wife taking care of them properly? Was she good to them? Ruth had been kind but reserved. Eloise hadn't stayed long enough to get to know her.

A wave of homesickness washed over her. Not for the cramped apartment with three and four children to a bedroom. Not for her father, who couldn't even keep their names straight. Not for the loud neighbors or long hours cleaning, cooking, and sewing for nine siblings. She longed for those rare, quiet moments at the end of an evening when the young ones went to bed, and her father worked late.

Her mother would sit in the rocker, quietly humming while darning socks or sewing on a button. They would talk about the days before Mama was married and her dreams of becoming an actress. Now, Eloise shared those dreams. Her mind wandered back to one fateful night.

"I'VE GOT an emergency fund hidden away," Mama said one night just before the New Year. "When the time is right, we'll send you to Hollywood. You have talent. The drama teacher told me so after the Christmas play."

"I can't take money away from the family," she had said without hesitation, though her heart pounded a little faster with the thought. "What if someone gets sick? Daddy would never allow it anyway."

"Your father doesn't know about it, and you won't tell him." Never taking her eyes off the sock she was darning, her calloused fingers pushed and pulled the needle and thread through the old material with skill and speed. "He doesn't understand women and their hopes and desires. He thinks they are just for breeding and keeping his house."

"But what if I'm not good enough? What if I waste your savings and never make it?" She heard the excitement mixed with panic in her voice. Could this even be a possibility? Her hands shook as she finished the button and broke the thread with her teeth. "I couldn't face you again."

"Of course you could. I'm your mother." Mama's urgent tone

12

made Eloise look up. "It doesn't matter whether you're successful. The important thing is to chase that dream and have no regrets. Don't be me. You deserve better."

ONE MONTH LATER, Mama came down with a fever that kept her in bed. Her father had grudgingly called the doctor after a week. Pneumonia. She took her last breath a few days later. Looking around the bedroom at the family crowded close to the bed, Eloise had never felt so alone. The younger children cried; the older ones seemed lost and confused.

Her three eldest sisters were married with families of their own. Her two older brothers had enlisted, one in the army and one in the navy. Eloise would have to see to the three youngest.

How could she take Mama's place?

Fate stepped in. At the end of February, her father brought home Ruth. Eloise was sure the cool look, when Daddy introduced her as his new wife, had meant to be intimidating. The "how nice to meet you" really meant "I'll be the woman of the house from now on." It worked.

On her eighteenth birthday, she pried up the floorboard inside the kitchen pantry and found Mama's emergency fund. Three days later, she stepped off a bus in sunny Los Angeles. It had been her first trip outside her neighborhood, let alone the state. And the City of Angels was a paradise compared to her home.

Even in March, the sun shone every day, although some days through a haze of smog. The only view she'd seen in Chicago on a regular basis was the apartment buildings on the South Side. Now, she could take a trolley car or bus and smell the fresh salt air of the Pacific Ocean or see distant mountaintops. She'd never have to worry about darning a winter coat again. The first time she saw the Hollywood sign, her mother's voice had whispered in her ear, *Chase that dream and have no regrets.*

The women at the local YWCA had found her a room at a boarding house.

"The landlady is strict, but you'll be safe there. No hanky-panky in her establishment, and the breakfast is plentiful. You'll get at least one good meal a day."

They bombarded her with advice before sending her off to Henley's House for Ladies. She must have carried an invisible sign, advertising: *Eager beaver here.*

"Don't tell a possible employer you're an actress. They don't trust movie people to be dependable."

"With that blonde hair, blue eyes, and those curves, you should be able to find a job. Do remember to smile—men expect it around here—but sweetly, not flirty-like. They'll get the wrong idea."

"If you're asked to audition in a private office with a couch, *run*. Don't be bamboozled."

Their voices clanged like fire engine bells in her head. Do this, don't do that. It scared the applesauce out of her, but they meant well. Some of their instructions had been helpful as she made her way through unfamiliar city streets. Unfortunately, Eloise had not been prepared for the cost of living in California, and her money went quickly. Her savings had been enough to cover two months' rent in advance.

Yesterday, her landlady met her at the door for the September payment.

"It's only the end of August," she had said in a reasonable tone. "I have another week."

"Just letting you know where you stand, girlie. If you don't have it on the first, you better have your bags packed. Or I'll pack them for you." Mrs. Henley's bark was worse than her bite on most matters but not when it came to money. "I've been stiffed too many times."

The lifeguard's shrill whistle brought her back to Sunset Pier. Eloise stood and brushed the sand from her legs and flapped her soggy hem, then slid her flats back on her damp feet. Checking her watch, she hurried toward the trolley to catch the next Red Car heading back into the city. With one last deep breath of the fresh ocean breeze, she smiled and thought of her upcoming audition.

Maybe tomorrow will be the day. Maybe tomorrow I'll get noticed.

CHAPTER 2

Los Angeles
September 1950

*T*he room spun. Eloise grabbed for the edge of the table as the coffee slipped from her grasp and her knees buckled. Her legs turned to noodles, and she closed her eyes, preparing to meet the unforgiving cement floor. Instead, strong arms wrapped around her waist and under her knees.

"Hey there, doll. Looks like you need a little help." His smoky gray eyes sent rejuvenating warmth through her body. Her skin tingled where it touched his, and her stomach did a flip.

"I... I think I just need something to eat. Once I get through the next number, I'll be fine."

"Well, trust me. If you faint in the middle of the dance routine, you won't have to worry about being called back. Extras are a dime a dozen." The deep, rich timbre of his voice soothed her nerves. His breath tickled, his mouth so close to her ear. "Let's see what I can scrounge up. You weigh about as much as the script I just finished."

The dizziness returned as he set her back down, but his arm remained around her waist. She leaned on him for support, embarrassment keeping her gaze on her worn, black tap shoes.

"And what shall I call my knight in shining armor?" she asked as her eyes strayed to the well-manicured fingers resting on her belt and the unadorned ring finger. "I take it you're a writer?"

"Yes, ma'am. Ross Wilson at your service." He tipped an imaginary hat. "And the princess in distress?"

"Eloise Kolby." She took a chance and looked up at her hero. The slate-colored eyes moved from her head to her nylon-clad legs, then very slowly back up to her chest. Her scant costume seemed little protection against his leisurely inspection. The heat began in her neck and rose. "I need this job. The landlady says she takes cash not excuses."

"Well, everyone needs a roof over his head. Tell her you're working on the set of *The African Queen* with Humphrey Bogart and Katharine Hepburn. Maybe she'll give you a break in the hopes of an autograph." He gave her a wink, sending her stomach into another tumble.

"I've had a crush on Bogie since I was a little girl." A giggle erupted at the thought. "Ha! Could you imagine working on the same set as either of them? Unfortunately, Mrs. Henley doesn't believe you can deposit an autograph in the bank. I had to pay rent or eat this week."

A ham sandwich magically appeared in Ross's free hand. He guided her to a stool, and she sank onto it, accepting the food with thanks. Another crewmember approached with a script in hand. The two men spoke quietly with their heads bent over the paper. She watched her new friend as he gestured, his hands animated with the conversation.

He was not tall, but his stocky build made him appear as large as the other man. Definitely the artist type with his casual slacks, barely tucked shirt, and longer hair. His ash-blond curls looked as if his fingers raked through them more often than a comb. A deep chuckle made the other man smile. Ross slapped him on the back, then nodded in her direction. They both turned to study her.

"The blonde?" the man asked. "She's a looker, all right. Sure, I'll see what I can do. Is she available at night?"

"Can you work in the evening?"

"Me?" she asked around a mouthful of sandwich. "Tell me a time and I'll be there. I mean... what kind of job is it?"

Maybe the precious money spent on her hair had been worth it. One director had told her to get rid of the long tresses and look more like Marilyn Monroe. She'd compromised with a shoulder-length cut and brightened her sandy brown to a deep blonde.

"An extra for a Minnelli film. I worked on the script for his last one, *Father of the Bride*. That's how I met this wise guy." Ross thumbed his friend next to him. "The choreographers need to add another number and want the girls to get in some late-night practices. We can't fall behind schedule. Jack says he can get you in."

Jack opened his mouth as if to argue, then looked at her with a sigh. "Can you sing too?"

Before Eloise could answer, he held up a hand. "Of course you can. You can do anything a director asks, right?"

She smiled and wondered how many girls came to Hollywood with stars in their eyes. Hundreds, she supposed. Naïve and hopeful, most of them ended up back home or slinging plates in a shabby LA diner. If they were lucky, they got bit parts in a background cast with twenty-five other girls kicking up their legs in unison. If they were really lucky, they got a one-liner and a close-up.

Eloise had not been so fortunate—yet. Leaving her home in Chicago six months ago, she'd already been a clerk in a department store, a secretary for an overly friendly PI, and still served burgers at a local joint near her apartment. Waitressing worked best because she could trade shifts to accommodate Hollywood's crazy schedule. It was hard to keep a job when you took off for auditions or played stand-in for a sick extra. Dozens of would-be actresses waited to snatch up anything that was available, and flexibility was key.

"Be back here at six tomorrow night, Lot Two, near the New England set," the taller man said with a shake of his head and a sideways glance at Ross. "Don't know how you can keep up, pal."

"Thanks, Jack." He chuckled and winked again at Eloise. "It's all in the smile."

The call sounded for the dancers to return, and she stood up. "Gosh, pennies from heaven. How can I thank you?"

"Have dinner with me. I'll wait for you to get off and buy you a real meal." He stepped in closer, bending slightly to whisper in her ear, "Anything your gorgeous heart desires."

The pulse in her temple pounded as the blood rushed to her head again. But this time her lightheadedness wasn't due to lack of food or sleep. He smelled of suntan lotion and tobacco, and she somehow knew that scent would be forever linked to this man. Suddenly shy, she nodded and headed back to join the group of dancers. His eyes drilled a hole into her back as she walked away from him.

"It's about time, girly," yelled one of the choreographers from the other side of the set. "We ain't paying you by the hour, ya know."

As she fell into the steps of the routine, Eloise dared a look back at Ross. The man sank his hands deep into his pockets and smiled. An unhurried, sexy, dimpled smile. He turned and walked away, taking her heart with him.

* * *

FOUR HOURS LATER, she bent over her knees, panting as if she'd just run across the entire MGM studio. She hoped that man really did have her heart because the one in her chest felt like it would explode.

"A bit out of shape, eh?"

Eloise looked up to see Rita Hayworth's twin grinning down at her. The burnished copper hair and teasing blue eyes did not help her mood. How could someone look like that after an afternoon of such torture?

"It's been a few weeks since I've been on a dance set. I'll be fine." With forced energy, she pushed off her knees and straightened to her full height. "But tell me we are done for today."

With a husky laugh, she agreed. "Yes, ma'am. Officially off duty!"

"Who's hungry?" called a voice from the group of girls. A jumbled chorus of "me" and "I am" echoed over the now quiet set. Eloise searched the lot for Ross.

"If you're waiting for Wilson, don't. He's as popular as soda at a fountain, and everyone wants a drink of him." The redhead put an arm around her shoulder and gave a squeeze. "C'mon out with us, honey. My treat. You look like you need a good meal without owing some Romeo for it."

"But Ross said he'd pick me up—"

"I bet he did. Do you believe everything people tell you?" She put a hand on her hip and took a pose like her mother used to when she'd done something foolish. "This is the movie business, sweetie. Don't go flipping your wig over every sweet-talking man you meet. They're like ants at a picnic."

Tears burned at the back of her eyes. Had she really been that naïve? He seemed so sincere. "I guess... I really am hungry."

"Atta girl. Stick with me. I've been around the block a few times. The name's Sally. Sally Berkeley." She held out her hand. "And no, I'm *not* related to Busby Berkeley. If I were, I wouldn't be selling myself for a few bucks a day on this B-rated movie. I'd be a star, dahling."

"Hi Sally, I'm Eloise Kolby," she replied with a laugh. "It's nice to meet you. I'd love to tag along, but I insist on buying my own."

They left the lot and walked out behind a group of extras. "Hey, Lucy, how about the usual?" someone yelled.

"Just where I was headed. I can smell that barbecue from here," answered the faceless voice as the crowd passed under the MGM gate and out onto the street.

"Where are we going?"

"A little joint my uncle owns. He's got the best sauce in LA and the coldest beer." Sally hooked arms with her. "And you've probably earned both today."

Twenty minutes later, Eloise sat with five hoofers, a make-up artist, and a studio secretary. The conversation was nonstop, and she had no idea how they understood one over the other. But for the first time in six months, she wasn't lonely. She hadn't realized how much she missed the noise of her large family, and the raucous laughter cheered her soul. The smell of barbecue chicken signaled a rumble from her stomach and made her mouth water. "This is enough food for three meals," she said in surprise. It was a banquet compared to the free blue plate special they got after a long shift at the diner.

"I've got connections, honey," Sally said as she licked her

fingers with a loud smacking noise. "Ready for another beer?"

"Oh gosh, no," she said with a giggle. "One is making me silly enough."

"So where did you come from, and how long have you been here?"

"Chicago and six months," she answered dutifully, trying to keep a serious expression. To her relief, the group hooted and snorted.

"We aren't the coppers, honey. Just getting to know you," one of the girls said. "What other acting jobs have you had so far?"

"*Hmph.* If you call them acting, then I've been part of a crowd at an ice rink, a girl in the middle pew of a church, part of a roaring audience at a football game—"

"So you've made quite a name for yourself, eh?" Sally raised her glass. "To the golden ring. May we grab it before we're old and gray."

The mugs clinked together as the waitress checked on them. "Can I get you ladies anything else?"

"A leading role, a rich man, and a new pair of kicks," said a girl named Jessy. "Wait, if I'm the leading role, I don't need the rich man."

"And if you have a rich man, you don't need the leading role," answered Sally as she clinked another glass. "What's next, ladies?"

"Bed for me," said Eloise, stifling a yawn. "I have to work an early shift tomorrow and be back at the lot by six."

"What's the movie?" asked the waitress.

"It's…" Thrilled with another dancing job, she'd forgotten to ask.

"Who's the director?"

"Vincent Minnelli."

The group *oohed* and *ahhed* appropriately. "I bet Romeo

set it up for her." Sally covered the side of her mouth with her hand and whispered loudly to the other girls. "Ross Wilson."

This time it was a chorus of moans.

"I thought he was very nice," Eloise said, defending the man who'd saved her from injury and fed her a sandwich. "Although he did stand me up."

"Consider yourself lucky." The secretary leaned in with a grin. "I hear all his conquests eventually end up in his scripts."

Twenty minutes later, Eloise walked up from the subway and headed toward Pershing Square. It was a lovely little park in the middle of the business district. Her feet hurt, so she took a moment to sit on a bench, partly lit by the lights of the Paramount Theater across the street.

A tickle went up her leg, and she slapped at the bug. A tiny scream escaped as her fingers touched fur. Then a p-u-r-r-r-r-r. A black, brown, and orange striped cat wrapped itself in and out of her legs. On the top of its head was a pumpkin-shaped spot.

"Well, aren't you an odd duck? I mean, cat!" She reached down and scratched its head. "And how is the little punkin-head tonight?"

Reaching into her bag, Eloise pulled out a piece of the barbecue chicken and shared it with her new feline friend. The loud meows told her that had not been a wise decision. She really was a dumb Dora.

"You'll probably try to follow me home now." As she walked away, her prediction proved correct. The cat loped behind her, stopping occasionally to sniff at a wrapper on the ground or bat at something that blew by. "If I had my own place, I'd keep you. Really, I would. But Mrs. Henley frowns enough as it is."

The cat stared up at her as she opened the door to the

boarding house. "One more bite," she said with a smile, tossing a sauce-soaked chunk down to the cat. "Night, Punkinhead."

* * *

SHE HURRIED under the huge MGM gate, the carved lion spying down at her as she ran. Her square heels echoed against the pavement as she jogged past the closed offices of the studio and searched for signs of life in Lot Two. A group of people gathered ahead, chatting easily outside another building. She slowed her pace; it wouldn't do her any good to start work in a sweat.

A voice called out just as she joined the others. "If you are here for a dance extra, see Jillian on the right. If you are part of the café scene, go to the left and see Bob."

Both held clipboards and began checking off names. Eloise approached the woman.

"Name?"

"Eloise Kolby."

The woman moved her pencil down the paper, then back up again. "I don't have you on here. Who sent you?"

"Ross Wilson and a man called Jack."

"Oh, one of RW's girls. I see." She looked over the line of workers and yelled, "Hey, where's Jack?"

"I'm over here. What do you need?" Jack emerged from behind the extras, cleaning his glasses with a handkerchief. "Oh, hiya, doll."

Jillian rolled her eyes. "She says you and RW sent her over. Is she café or hoofer?"

The man turned his attention to Eloise. "You're the sheba with the nice gams. Ross sure can pick 'em." He looked back at Jillian. "She's dancin'."

Two hours and at least a bucket of sweat later, someone

called for a break. A table had been set up with refreshments, and bodies crowded around to grab a sandwich or a drink. Eloise held back, waiting for a space to open up.

She felt him first. A quiet presence behind her, followed by a familiar whisper in her ear. Her stomach quaked in a good way, little moths fluttering around and tickling her insides. "Still think the job is pennies from heaven? Or are you earning your keep?"

Without turning, she answered, "If tonight is pennies, I think a dime would kill me."

A familiar pair of tanned hands wrapped around her waist from behind, warm lips brushing the side of her head as he spoke, "Then we won't up the ante."

She stiffened, unaccustomed to such an intimate touch from a stranger.

"Don't tell me you're a fuddy-duddy?" The words teased, but the tone stroked and caressed, easing her back into his chest. She struggled to come up with something smart to say, but his voice dripped over her and stole any conscious thought. "Good. I'd like to take you out for a late dinner tonight."

Common sense smacked her in the face. In a pleasant tone, she replied, "I'd love to, but it will be hard to surpass our date from last night."

"But we didn't—" Ross put his hands on her shoulders and spun her around until they were face to face. "Please accept my apology. A business meeting went way over, and by the time I made it back here, you were gone. I had no idea how to call or find you so... here I am now."

"Here you are," she repeated, wondering how her voice sounded so nonchalant. Her legs had that rubbery feeling again. Those hazy gray eyes sent a chill and heat through her body at the same time. "It will take a lot to make it up to me."

"I can't think of a better way to spend the rest of my night."

* * *

DECEMBER 1950

Ross was everything a leading man should be: handsome, charming, intelligent, and talented. Over the next few months, he wined and dined her and introduced her to a multitude of names she would never remember. It seemed no matter where they went, classy restaurant or cheesy diner, dance hall or dive, people knew Ross Wilson.

"It's all about the connections, baby doll. If you don't know the Glitterati, how will you clinch the deal?" he explained one night at a crowded dance hall off Sunset Boulevard. "You never know who will put you in line for the big one. So I make sure I leave no stone unturned if you get my meaning."

With his smile and charisma, Eloise doubted he had to put forth much effort. Women flocked to him, and she often had to remind herself, even though they were a couple, he had not hinted at anything long-term. She hoped that would change soon.

"What'll you have?" the waitress yelled over the noise of the band.

"I'll have a Manhattan, and the lady will take a white wine spritzer." Ross smiled, showing his dimples, and slipped a bill on the girl's tray. "Don't get lost on the way back."

They had stopped in for a nightcap after the theater. "What did you think of the movie?" Eloise asked, leaning in close so she could hear his response. "I love John Wayne westerns."

"No one can sling a gun like the Duke," Ross answered distractedly, inspecting the crowd.

"Are you looking for someone?" She scanned the bodies, twisting and swinging around the dance floor. "Anyone I know?"

"Nah, just thought a friend of mine said he might bring his date here. I wanted to talk to him about a storyline." He moved his hat to the other side of the small table and took her hand. "Did I tell you how lovely you look tonight?"

Eloise blushed. "No, and don't stop now."

"Is the dress new? The dark navy makes your hair look like spun gold." He reached up and pushed a stray wave behind her ear, the back of his hand lingering against her jaw. "Your skin is soft as butter."

"The dress is Sally's, but the hair and skin are all mine." She covered his hand with her own.

"Here you go," said the waitress as she set the drinks down in front of them. "Enjoy. I'll be by to check on you later." She pursed her lips at Ross, and the corners of her mouth turned up before moving on to the next table.

"Are you sure you don't know her?" She hated the suspicious tone in her voice. *Stop it. I am his date. He took me to the movie, and he's bringing me home, not the waitress.*

"Not that I remember."

"What are you working on now?" A change of subject would be best. "Didn't you finish that musical?"

"Yeah. A buddy asked me to help with a project he's starting. Guess who the director is?"

"Oh, I'm no good at this. Just tell me. Is it someone big?" The excitement in his eyes gave it away.

"Billy Wilder." The grin on his face was infectious. "If I can get my own script in front of him…"

"Oh, Ross, this is so exciting. What an opportunity." She squeezed his hand and leaned over to place a kiss on his cheek. "For luck."

"Luck has nothing to do with it. It's all in who you know."

"Well, a little luck certainly can't hurt. I need a powder break. I'll be right back." Weaving her way between tables, she headed to the ladies' room. Billy Wilder. She hoped Ross found a spot for her too.

On her way back to the table, she heard a familiar laugh and turned toward the sound. She recognized a girl who had worked with her on a previous set. Alice was a top-heavy blonde who wore a signature red lipstick on her plump mouth and had a pronounced whine to her voice. Her hands slid up and down the man's chest, just inside his jacket lapels. The fake black lashes batted up at him with a furious flutter. Leaning down, the man said something, and Alice laughed again, then pulled on his tie and gave him a smack on the lips.

Eloise shook her head at the woman's brazen actions and walked back to their table. Ross was gone. Odd, maybe he had to use the restroom too. She sipped her drink and waited. It was not unusual for him to see an acquaintance and disappear for a quarter of an hour. She felt his strong hands on her back a few moments later as he pulled her coat over her shoulders.

"What do you say we call it a night?" Ross yawned. "I have a big day tomorrow. And I think I found you a part for next week. Another musical. Are you up for it?"

"Like you said, never turn down an opportunity."

The drive home was quiet. Just the soft voice of Perry Como over the radio and the purr of the old Chevy while she snuggled up against his shoulder. He pulled up in front of the three-story brownstone where she now shared an apartment with Sally.

"Tell Red I got you home by curfew." His sardonic tone made her grimace. There was no love lost between her best friend and her boyfriend. They were both polite to each other, but conversation was limited to sarcastic banter and one-liners. On the big screen, it might have been laughable. In her living room, it grew tiresome playing the peacemaker.

"She's on a date herself. I doubt I'll see her before morning." A dim light shone in the second-floor window. "Only the lamp is on. It'll just be me and Punkinhead with a bowl of warm milk and a good book I've been trying to finish."

"I can't believe you brought that stray cat with you. You have a good heart, Eloise."

"Well, we were both alone in a big city. I'm surprised she hung around so long at the boarding house. I guess no one else saved scraps for her. I'm a dependable meal ticket." She had spent many nights sitting out on the front steps of Mrs. Henley's Establishment for Ladies, with only Punkin to talk to about her day.

Her shyness kept her from making friends easily. She supposed that was why she had been drawn to Sally and Ross. They both had larger-than-life personalities, and it allowed her to remain in the background yet enjoy the excitement of large events. Eloise, with her quiet, unassuming way, just blended into the crowd. She was quite happy to watch the action and let her friends take center stage.

Ross walked her up the stairs to her apartment. She unlocked the door and leaned against the frame. As he bent to kiss her goodnight, the glow from the table lamp fell on his shirt collar. She spotted a smudge of lipstick. Bright red lipstick.

"Tired, are you?" she asked as she used her thumb to rub the cherry spot off his shirt. Tears burned her eyes; hurt and anger battled one another to get control. "How could you?"

"What… Oh, I can explain—"

"I saw her, but your back was turned. Sally is right, isn't she? You're just a drugstore cowboy with a girl on every corner." She turned her back on him, ready to throw herself on her bed for a good, long cry.

"Doll, she threw herself at me. I felt sorry for her. She's just a dame with no class. You're my girl." He grabbed her arm and pulled her back. "You know that, don't you?"

"How would I? You call on Wednesdays, and we go out every Saturday night. I have no idea what you do the rest of the week." Hot tears fell down her cheeks, embarrassment and insecurity rising to the surface in front of this self-assured man of the world. Had she really thought she could hold his interest?

"Because I'm telling you. You're my best girl and don't forget it." He tipped her chin up with a finger. "Who do I take to the important parties? Who do I introduce to my friends?"

She sniffed. "I suppose." Her heart wanted to believe him so badly. Being on his arm made her feel important without being scrutinized. Growing up, her father's attention had been critical or absent. With Ross, she felt special just by association.

"Who do I want to meet my parents when they come for Christmas?"

She gasped. "Your parents are coming? I thought they'd never visit Sin City." Ross came from a very conservative, old Southern family. "And you want them to meet me?"

"Of course. Like I said, you're my best girl." He leaned down and kissed her softly on the mouth. "Now go get some sleep, and I'll call you on Wednesday. Okay?"

She nodded, her mind spinning with possibilities. She couldn't wait to tell Sally. He moved quickly down the flight of stairs two at a time, obviously catching a second wind.

"You don't really believe him, do you?" Her best friend's cynical tone floated out into the hall.

"I thought you were on a date." She stepped inside and

locked the door. "And yes, I am not as distrustful as you. He has to have feelings for me if I'm to meet his parents."

"Well, he can't introduce them to some floozy. You'll make them believe their son is staying on the good, moral high road." Sally peeled herself off the couch, the flowing print skirt clinging to her long, slender legs. "He needs a nice girl to make himself look reputable. But he's not the marrying kind."

"I think you're wrong. Deep down, he wants love just like I do."

"Oh, he wants love all right. All kinds of it. He said you're his *best* girl, not his *only* girl." She stopped, and concern filled her narrowed blue eyes. "This business is too cutthroat for you, my sweet, darling friend. You deserve someone who adores you, who can't wait to see you at the end of the day. A man who thinks that his world will stop revolving if you walk out of it."

Eloise's lips trembled. "You deserve that too, you know."

"Aw, honey." Sally wrapped her in a big hug. "Of course I do. And I'll get it because I won't settle for less. And that's what you have to do. Not ever settle for less."

"You don't think I can make it here, do you?"

"I think the movie industry will end up sucking the life from you, and I hate to see it. You have so much more talent than I do. Your voice, your dancing, all outshines mine." She stood back and held Eloise at arm's length. "But I have the thick skin and a smart mouth. I can stand up for myself."

The past nine months had been so much harder than she had expected. Her confidence had grown, but Sally was right. Center stage, being in the fish bowl, scared the heck out of her.

"I can't go back to Chicago. I just can't." Her voice cracked. "Daddy would laugh and tell me I was as stupid as my mother." Punkinhead let out a howl and began rubbing against her leg. She stooped and picked her up, hiding her shame in the cat's fur.

"Oh, you're not getting rid of me that easy. You just need a plan in case this doesn't work out. And it can't rely on Romeo. Deal?"

"Deal. I've been thinking about teaching. I love children, and it's the only thing I miss from back home. Maybe I could give music and dance lessons." Eloise took a deep breath, her natural optimism returning. "I'll give it two years. If I don't consider myself a success by then, I'll try a different direction."

Chase your dream. Have no regrets.

"Atta girl. Now let's have some hot cocoa, and I'll tell you about my awful date. First, he showed up with a friend, honking his horn under our window…"

CHAPTER 3

September 1952
Los Angeles

*E*loise untied the apron, laid it on the back of a kitchen chair, and checked her watch. Just past five and a little over two hours to finish dinner and get dressed. She turned on the radio and sang along with Louis Armstrong, *"Sweetheart, I ask no more than this..."*

Punkinhead followed her into the bedroom, purring along to the song. She picked her up and rubbed her ears. "Sometimes it's hard to believe how far we've come in two years. I couldn't have asked for better roommates." Though Sally continued to put up a squawk about her feline companion, Eloise often caught the two of them curled up for a nap. Eloise had explained how she'd met them both the same night and been feeding Punkin every day since. Red might put up a tough front, but she had a big heart.

"Now, let's hope Mr. Wilson is as understanding." Her

voice fell silent as she looked at the meager contents of her closet. Tonight, she would be a leading lady, so to speak, and needed a ritzy dress to look the part. Ross had been excited all week but refused to tell her why. When he called to say he was taking her somewhere special tonight, her heart leapt.

"I have a surprise for you, baby doll. Make sure you're all decked out." When she pushed him for more information, he had laughed and said, "Just be ready at seven. We're doing the town tonight!"

The front door opened with a bang. "Elli, Elli are you here?" Sally barged into the bedroom, breathless. "I've got a letter."

"From George? Is he okay?"

"Oh, honey, he's more than okay. He's coming home." She pushed the thick, red hair from her face and folded her hands together as she looked up to the ceiling. "I'm not a praying woman, but for that man, I'd do anything. And I did. Thank you, Lord."

Sally had met George just before the Korean War broke out. She had sprained her ankle on a set and gone to the Los Angeles County hospital. It had been quite a chase, but the determined intern had finally caught his girl. When Eloise had met him at a New Year's Eve party, she'd felt like they had been friends for years.

Three months later, he had been drafted as a medic. The girls had filled his care packages, shopped for his favorite nonperishables, and taken countless pictures, sent to keep him from forgetting Sally. The poor soldier didn't stand a chance. The couple had written almost weekly but had not seen each other in over eighteen months. George had written last month that he was being transferred to the States for the rest of his term, working with the veterans who'd received amputations during their service.

"He says he'll be close to home by the time I get this...

34

Holy moly, that's next week. I've got to pack. I'm going to Nevada."

She flew past her roommate, the monologue continuing as she opened dresser drawers and threw shirts and lingerie over her head, then froze. The silence in the room unnerved Eloise. It was never quiet when Red was home.

Sally turned and sat on the bed. Tears streamed down her cheeks; her shoulders quaked. Eloise ran to the bed and threw her arms around the crying woman. She rocked her back and forth, making soothing shushing noises.

"He kept his promise. He really kept his promise." She wept into Eloise's blouse. "I was so afraid he would die over there. We'd barely had any time together."

"*Shhhh.* It's all right now. He's coming home." Her eyes blinked back tears as she felt the sobs of relief go through her friend's body. "This is a happy time."

"I know. I've fought so hard to stay positive the past eighteen months because if I didn't... And you! You kept me sane while I waited. R.W. will always hold a tiny but special place in my heart for standing you up that first night. We may not have become friends."

"Wouldn't Ross love to be a fly on the wall. He thinks you hate him."

"I do. He's a sorry, cheating you-know-what. And you'd be better off without him." Sally picked up a pair of clean underwear next to her and blew her nose. "Someday you'll see him for what he is, but in the meantime, I'll be looking out for you."

"And what's this talk about Nevada?"

"George wants me to meet his mother before we get married. I'll go to her place in Nevada, then we'll come back here, and he'll pick up where he left off but at a military hospital."

"Married? You're getting married? Oh, Sally." She

35

squeezed her tight. "I'm so happy for you. But Nevada? I'll miss your wedding."

"I'll make it up to you, honey."

Eloise looked at her watch and gasped. "Oh, the time. I have to get ready. You're not the only one being proposed to, you know."

"*Hmph*! Ross isn't the marrying kind."

She told Sally of his behavior the past week, then begged her for a dress to wear. "Only because I love you. I wouldn't do this for him."

The next forty-five minutes flew by as more clothes went flying, the Solo Red Top curlers came out, and a pair of stockings found without a run. The image now staring back at her glowed with satisfaction.

"How did you do this?" Eloise asked in awe. "Even with the curlers still in my hair, I look gorgeous." She twirled from side to side as the long skirt fell into natural pleats over the crinoline beneath, swaying just below her knees. The burnt-orange print made a bold statement and showed off her blonde waves. A tight-fitting bodice pushed her breasts up and added cleavage she didn't know existed.

"Sit down and let me take those curlers out and add some makeup." It was an order—Sally rarely requested. "Let's see. A little eyeliner, some mascara... Where did my eyelash curler go?"

She smiled as her friend searched through her box of goodies. "Ah, here it is. Add some coral lipstick and *voila*! A man would be crazy not to propose to you now!"

Both women stood back and admired the images smiling back. It was bittersweet. They were getting the men they wanted but wouldn't be together for that precious memory. As if on cue, Sally turned and gave her a ferocious hug. "If he doesn't do the right thing, I'll sic George on him when we get back!"

She stepped back and a loud *meow* broke the moment. "Oh, poor Punkinhead. Are you all right?" Eloise stooped and picked up the cat, rubbing the orange spot on top of her head. "Look, Punkin. We almost match!" The spot on the cat's head was close to the print in the dress. The feline began to purr and rub her head against her owner's chest.

"Enough of that. No fur on *my* clothes, best friend or not."

After a quick dinner, they tuned the radio to Gene Autrey's "Melody Ranch." A voice came through the crackle: "*Brought to you by Wrigley Spearmint Gum and Wrigley Doublemint.*"

"Maybe one of our future husbands will buy us a television," Sally said with a sigh. "Betty has one. It's just like a little movie screen in your own living room. We're invited on Monday to watch 'I Love Lucy.'"

The girls sat on the sofa, listening to the cowboy's nasal tone sing about love in the Old West. Eloise wondered how her roommate could manage to look so glamorous in jeans and a tucked-in blouse. Those glorious auburn curls rebelled against the bandana wrapped around her head and spilled out beneath the knot on the top. Her hand strayed to her own ear and tucked a short wave behind it. Would Sally give up her career now that she was getting married?

At precisely 7:30 p.m., a knock sounded at the door. Eloise jumped up, feeling more nervous than she'd expected. Rushing to the door, she opened it a crack and peeked through. There stood Ross, in pleated dark slacks and a crisp white shirt that showed off his tan, holding a mixed bouquet of flowers. The door opened wide.

"Oh, my. They're beautiful," she exclaimed, reaching for the colorful bundle. She dared a sideways glance toward the living room. Sally raised her eyebrows as if impressed.

"They don't compare to my gal." Ross gave a whistle as he grabbed her by the waist and swung her around. "Only the best frolic pad for you tonight, baby doll. Ready for a night on the town?"

"You betcha," she answered, his mood contagious. "You won't call me a flat tire tonight! Where are we going?"

"I'm in the mood for a little dancing. Your carriage awaits you." He headed toward the door, then paused, looking over his shoulder. "Um, did you care to join us?"

"The sincerity in your voice puts a tear in my eye but no thanks. The radio and I have a date tonight while I start packing." Sally's tone was as syrupy sweet as molasses. "You two have a ball."

Ross practically dragged her down the stairs. When they got to the street, Eloise stopped, mouth wide open. "Where did you get this?" she asked as he opened the passenger door of a burgundy wine-colored Ford. The heavy chrome shone brightly under a street lamp.

"I borrowed it from a buddy. It's a 1947 V-8 Super Deluxe. She's spiffy, ain't she?" His chest seemed to puff out as he helped her inside the cream-colored interior. "I'll have one of my own before long, don't you worry."

"Do you have a new project coming up?" He always treated himself to something new whenever he began work on a new movie or sold one of his scripts. "It must be quite a deal."

"Well, as a matter of fact, that is one thing I wanted to talk to you about. But we'll save the best for last. First, scoot on over here. You're too far away." He patted the seat next to him, then pulled out an envelope and handed it to her.

She obliged and opened the envelope while he played with the radio dial.

"Ross, you've inherited a house?"

"Yessiree. Thank you, great-aunt-whoever-Wilson." He leaned over and gave her a kiss on the cheek. "It's in some two-bit town up north called Ridgecrest."

"Her name was Mona. Your father's sister, I assume?"

"Yes, the family spinster. His oldest sister left the house to *Aunt Mona*, but she was pretty hairy, I mean, pretty old herself. So, she never did anything with it. Guess it's been sitting empty for over five years now." He glanced sideways at her. "What's that big, beautiful smile for?"

Her mind raced with the possibilities. A new project, a house outside of LA. Yes, this was the night. Many movie people kept homes outside the city. Excitement swelled in her belly, and she pressed her hands against it to calm the butterflies.

"Nothing," she answered, leaning her head against his shoulder as he drove. "Just happy to be out with you tonight."

Then another notion overshadowed the joy. *Will I be happy staying home and raising a family?* Truth be told, the whole acting experience hadn't been what she'd hoped—or what her mother would have wanted for her. But it had rescued her from a life without dreams and taught her she was a survivor. And she had given it two years. Maybe this was her new beginning—being a wife, having a family. There were so many possibilities for the future. *Thank you, Mama.*

"Anyway," he said, cutting into her thoughts. "I'm figuring that house has to be worth at least enough to buy a new car. We need some style on wheels, ya know?"

A twinge of regret shot through her. *What is wrong with me? He's proposing—who cares about an old, abandoned home?*

"I'm sure it will. This car makes me feel like royalty." She wiggled against the soft leather seats and laughed aloud at herself. This would be an evening she'd never forget.

Ross drove along Sunset Boulevard, then turned and headed north for a block. He found a parking space and walked around the car to help her out. "We're going to the Tailspin," he announced, pointing to a building across the street. "It's a little wacky but has the best dance contests in town. And the band is from New York City."

They walked up to the door, and a man asked to see their identification. He was a big, burly guy who looked as if his nose had been broken more than once. He checked Ross's with a grunt but spoke to Eloise as he handed back her card. "If he doesn't make you happy tonight, darlin', you come back and see ol' Lou." Then his mouth split into a huge grin, showing at least two gaps.

Ross just put his hand on her lower back and pushed her through the door. She giggled. "What kind of a place is this?"

"Just a Swing joint…with a bit of gambling upstairs," he said, catching her sideways glance. "It's fine. We're just dancing and having a few drinks."

The smoke in the place was so thick that she tried to wave it away with a hand. It smelled of stale beer and cigar smoke. It tickled her nose, but her hand was already tapping her leg to the beat. Ross looked so pleased, so she ignored the offensive scents and enjoyed the music.

Off to her left was an elongated bar and a bartender who looked slightly less intimidating than the bouncer. A couple with their heads together tried to talk over the band as they sipped a drink. Several other patrons, two men, and a lone woman, sat on stools watching the crowd and listening to the band.

As they moved past the customers on stools, Eloise's eyes adjusted, and she saw tables and a small dance floor. She'd heard of these places but never been to one. Sally had, of course. She liked to cut a rug every chance she got before George came along. Then her hoofing days had ended, and she had turned into a proficient correspondent. They found an empty table, and a waitress in a short dress and large breasts came to take their order.

"I want a Manhattan, and the lady will have a Singapore

Sling." Ross folded a bill into her hand, but his smile faded as he looked up at her.

"The first one's on me, honey," the girl said with a wink. "Thanks for *lunch* the other day."

"I thought you didn't have a job." He gave a quick glance at Eloise. "Um, this is, uh—" He looked embarrassed when he couldn't come up with her name.

"Don't worry about it, dearie. Just *grab* me whenever you need something, okay?"

She walked away, her tightly clad backside moving provocatively. Ross peeled his eyes off the waitress and looked sheepishly at Eloise. "She was trying to get on at the studio."

"Is she the one Sally saw you with at Canter's for lunch?" She felt foolish now, thinking how she'd insisted her roommate had been mistaken—again. It hadn't been the first time someone had made comments about other women, but Ross always had an explanation. She had just never seen "his explanations" in person before.

"I bet Sally forgot to tell you I wasn't alone with her, either. There was a full table with me from the set, and I happened to be sitting next to the empty chair. The woman walked up and asked to join us. Gave us a whole sob story about no money, rent due, and how she needed a job." He shrugged. "So I bought her lunch. What's the harm?"

A small voice in the back of her head said not to believe his gobbledygook, but she ignored it again. She knew firsthand he could be a generous Joe, and this wasn't the time for an argument. "Listen, let's just have fun. You can buy lunch for whoever you want, but tonight it's just about us, okay?"

"Sure thing. I knew you'd understand. You're a real trooper." He put his arm around the back of her chair and gave her a kiss. "That's what I love about you."

Her heart thumped. Yes, he loved her. Of course he did.

As they sipped on drinks, she decided to give him a jump-start. "What did you want to talk to me about?"

"Well, I wanted to ask you... Hey, the band is starting back up. Let's swing!" He grabbed her hand and pulled her onto the small dance floor.

It was a fast beat, and before she knew it, her heels were flying, and Ross was swinging her from side to side. He was an excellent dancer and in great shape, able to pick her up like she was a paper doll. It made her feel so petite. With such a crowded space, couples had to be careful not to bang into each other. There were stories of concussions and fights when a woman would get knocked down, and a drunken date felt obligated to defend her honor. But they made it back to their table without any casualties.

The evening flew by. Ross was in rare form, entertaining her with hilarious stories from his youth and the various sets he had worked on. He always surprised her with a new tale. They danced, talked, and drank. She finally put her hand up after a third round.

"Really, you'll have to carry me up the stairs if I have another," she giggled as he finished a laugh-out-loud tale involving Cary Grant. "I haven't had this much fun in months."

He took her hand. "I'm glad. I really am. Shall we go?"

The drive home was a comfortable silence except for the radio. Nat King Cole's gentle tones floated over them. Ross sang softly in her ear, "Unforgettable, that's what you are..."

She snuggled into his shoulder, a pleasant haze filling her brain. *This night is almost perfect,* she thought in her fuzzy state. But she'd forgotten something...

"Here we are," whispered Ross as he pulled the Ford to the curb in front of her apartment building. His head lowered as his mouth covered hers in a tender kiss. His lips, so soft and persuasive, opened hers. He tasted of sweet vermouth, and it made her feel all warm on the inside.

"Can we talk?" He broke away and took her hands in his. His face was so close she could feel his breath on her hair. A delicate shudder of anticipation passed through her body.

This is it. Of course he wouldn't want to propose in a dance hall. He needs a romantic, private moment. That's why he borrowed this car.

Eloise smiled up expectantly, holding her breath as she waited to hear the words. After two years, it was time.

"I've been offered a job on location. It's not being broadcast yet because the actors haven't been verified. But I would be working with Gregory Peck and Audrey Hepburn." He paused and squeezed her fingers. "I would be gone for a few months. Maybe even six."

A brick had fallen from the sky and dropped on her head. The pleasant mist vanished, and she was suddenly very sober. Surely, this couldn't be his news. Yet…

"I know this is sudden, but it's a great opportunity for both of us. It's all about connections. If I'm successful, your career could advance as well." His reasoning and pleading tone gave her hope.

"Are you asking me to come with you, then?" But the instant tightening of his grip gave her the answer before he opened his mouth. No, she was not part of this plan. She took a deep breath as panic slowly spread in her stomach. Unbidden tears burned her eyes as she fought to maintain control.

"Where are you going?" she asked, her voice wavering despite her effort.

"Rome." He touched her cheek and wiped it with his thumb. "Aw, honey, don't cry. With all this McCarthy communist business going on, it's a good time to skip town for a while. Another dozen hit the blacklist this week. That man is out to destroy the movie industry."

She shook her head, not trusting her voice.

"We'll be in touch, and when I get back—"

"Sally is getting married. George is coming home, and she leaves next week for Nevada. I can't afford this apartment without a roommate. I've had no steady job since I took that last bit part you got for me," she rambled, desperate to get upstairs and throw herself on her bed. "And I don't think I can do this alone." Her hands covered her face, sobs rising in her chest.

"I didn't know, sweetheart," he said in a soft, soothing voice as he brushed her hair from her face. "Maybe I can find you a roommate before I go."

She shook her head and took the handkerchief he offered her. "Oh Ross, I just thought that tonight you were going to... to..."

Silence. Then a heavy sigh. "*Ahh*, I see."

Her heart broke. She could almost hear the crack. He had never even considered a proposal. Sally had been right. He wasn't the marrying kind. Wanting to escape and have a good cry, she pulled away and scooted toward the passenger door.

"Wait! I have an idea." He grabbed her arm to gently pull her back. Reaching into his coat pocket, Ross pulled out the paper she had looked at earlier. "Why don't you go and check out this house for us? Find out what kind of condition it's in and get it ready for the market. Then when I get back, we'll talk about our future."

Eloise looked up, his smoky eyes dark and unreadable in the shadows of the car. Hope sprang within her, and the ache in her chest eased a bit. He had said "our future."

"Where is it again?"

"Let's see," he said, opening the letter with a loud crinkle.

His fingers moved down the paper. "Nineteen Ivy Lane in Ridgecrest, California. Sounds nice, don't you think? It's not a very big town. I've heard people are usually friendly in small towns."

Something about that address did appeal to her. Maybe it would be good for her to get away. If the house needed a lot of work, it would keep her mind off Ross's absence.

"I'll call the lawyer and find out what we need to do to set it up. He can put me in contact with local businesses to help you get the place in order," he continued, his tone persuasive. "I'll set you up with an account for expenses and keep you in groceries. What do you say?"

Eloise looked at the address again and had an image of a porch and picket fence. "Can I bring Punkinhead?"

CHAPTER 4

September 1952
Ridgecrest, California

*I*vy Lane wrapped around the back of the tiny town of Ridgecrest like the ribbon on top of a package. It was quaint, peaceful, and had escaped the boom-town-like atmosphere converging on the rest of the community. Victor Burnham appreciated the familiar vista as his gaze wandered down the block. With its desert backdrop and mountain caps dotting the sky, it rang of simpler times. This was where he would buy a house and raise a family. Older ranch-style homes lined the street, a few with a front porch or a second story, all with nice-sized yards.

He walked down this lane every day to deliver the mail and knew each resident, the name of their pet wagging a tail behind the fence, and every crack in the sidewalk. He'd given names to the occasional strays that tagged along his route during good weather. And the weather was nice most of the time, excluding the occasional rain or sandstorm, so he often had company.

Pausing in front of a vacant house, he pushed his mailbag off to the side and leaned against the picket fence. It needed paint and a new gate. The front steps sagged a bit, and he could almost hear the laughter of children running up onto the porch. Something about the placement of the windows and door always made him think the place smiled down at him.

Yes, 19 Ivy Lane was special. The little flower garden was in full bloom, and splashes of red, gold, orange, and blue spilled over the fence. It always amazed Victor that, sitting on the edge of the Mojave Desert, plants with such vibrant color could survive. There had been little rain over the winter, and the annuals had needed a bit of help. But the chrysanthemums, roses, sedums, and sunflowers thrived in the September sun. Blackbrush bushes dotted the horizon beneath tall clumps of galleta grass that swayed in the constant breeze.

He shaded his eyes with a hand and peered back up at the house. One faded blue shutter creaked precariously in the breeze, winking at the great old California Pepper tree that stood guard on the west side. The evergreen's long, drooping branches reminded him of a weeping willow, sad and lonely without a loving owner to tend the property. It had been one of the first trees planted in the area and needed a family to sit beneath it.

The realtor said when old Mrs. Jenkins died, she had left it to a sister out East. An agency had hired someone to do the yard work and keep an eye on the place. Victor often stopped by on Saturdays, tending to little things he noticed throughout the week. Five years later, it remained empty with no "For Sale" sign out front. Always a patient man, he knew one day it would be his. He felt it in his bones with a certainty like the coming of Christmas or the fresh buds of spring. Adjusting the leather strap on his carrier again, he made a mental note to trim a few branches and continued along his route with a whistle.

* * *

The jalopy cruiser sped along U.S. Highway 395 toward Indian Wells Valley, tumbleweeds and dust flying through the air. Once out of LA, the traffic had slowed dramatically. Only an occasional automobile made an appearance as a speck in the distance, going by in a blur, and then gone as if it had been a mirage. The Sierra Nevada mountain range lined their view to the west and nothing but desert stretched off to the east.

"It sure was nice of George's friend to loan me his car. Said it was the least he could do for a soldier coming home." Sally stretched out an arm and yawned. "I need another cup of coffee. It's a long way to George's house after I drop you off in Podunk."

"The name is—"

"I know, I know. George said there's a naval air weapons station near there at China Lake. The population swelled overnight a few years ago with the job opportunities. Lots of trailers and makeshift housing close to the base." The forced positive tone made Eloise smile. "Maybe you'll find yourself a service man to keep you occupied."

"Company is fine, but I don't need anyone to take Ross's place." She stared out at the mountain caps beginning to show on the eastern horizon.

"What's good for the gander is good for the goose."

"Another word and I'll jump out of this car. My death will be on your shoulders," Eloise countered with a chuckle.

"I know you're looking out for me, but I know what I'm doing."

"Said the mouse to the cat. Speaking of death," Sally said, pointing to a billboard on the right, proclaiming, *Gateway to Death*. "Is that supposed to be some kind of welcome sign?"

They both giggled. "I hope not. I bet it's alluding to Death Valley nearby. Kind of a morbid sense of humor, huh?"

Half an hour later, another road sign told them to turn right toward Ridgecrest. As they approached, a concentration of trees added rich accents of green to the landscape. Pines and oak trees waved a welcome over the housetops.

They stopped at Tom's Desert Service and filled up with gasoline. Sally made quite an impression on the attendant as he leaned in the window. Her windblown hair, coupled with the snug-fitting blouse, mesmerized the poor kid. He tried his best not to look inside the car as he washed the windshield but failed miserably. It took all she had not to laugh at him as he stuttered the total.

"Th-that'll be $2.60, please," the boy said with downcast eyes. "Ma'am."

"Ma'am? You think I look like a ma'am?" Sally's shocked eyes sent the poor kid into another stuttering lapse. His face went as pale as his sun-streaked hair.

"I apologize, ma'—"

"Miss, and don't worry about it." Eloise leaned over and handed the teenager several dollar bills. "My friend gets a little grumpy when she needs coffee. You go ahead and keep the change."

"Well, I hope that's Romeo's money," her friend said with a snort as she gave herself a quick inspection in the rearview mirror. "Ma'am. Can you believe that?"

It was Saturday, and the early morning sun shone brightly on the spotless glass as they took in their first view of Ridgecrest. Eloise looked down the tiny main street at well-kept storefronts, a few with flowers hanging outside, and thought "charming." Sally took in the same view and said, "Oh good gravy. I bet I could walk around this town in ten minutes."

"Stop it! It's not that small. Everything I might possibly need is right here. Look, there's a burger place. And across the street is... Victory Market, then Masten's Variety Store, a hardware store," she continued to name the businesses as they passed each one, "Rizzardini's Appliances, the Band Box —don't ask, I have no idea—oh, and a shoe store."

"You've got me. No place can be that bad if it has a shoe store." She looked in the rearview mirror. "Hey, why don't we stop in at that market and pick you up a few groceries and cleaning supplies. Then you won't have to venture out on your own for a while."

They each grabbed a basket and filled them with odds and ends: cleaning supplies, a Tuffy scrubber, a ham, French's mustard, some bread, Stokely's canned fruit and vegetables, and some Maxwell House instant coffee. On impulse, Eloise threw in some taffy and a couple of Hershey bars. The older woman at the register smiled sweetly and asked if they had husbands at the naval station. "No, just passing through," Sally said lightly.

It had been easy enough to find the main street, and they knew from the cashier's directions that Ivy Lane was at the end of it. Residents were already stirring with cars parked in front of a diner and the hardware store. Several people watched them with interest as they drove down the road. An old man sitting on a bench nodded and held up a hand in greeting.

"Are you sure you want to do this?" Sally looked doubt-fully at Eloise. "The old gal at Victory's had that gossipy look when we asked about the house. She'll be telling everyone two floozies just rode into town."

"Yes, I want to do this. And only one floozy rode into

town, thank you. Look, that old man is waving at us. That's what they do in small towns." Her voice sounded much more confident than she felt. "Ross has given me his trust and a decent budget. I need to get this house in order so he can sell it, and then I'll wait for his letter so I know what to do next."

A loud snort came from the driver's side. "Look, sweetie. We've been over this before. Word has it he's smooching up to one of the actresses who requested him for the project. If you can't read between the lines of that script, you need your head examined."

"He explained those were just rumors started by another writer jealous he didn't get the job." Eloise raised her chin, letting Sally know she was digging in her heels. "Ross loves me. He told me we would talk about *our* future as soon as he got back."

"Everyone knows he's all about connections and what *or who* will help him reach his goal. You are his pretty, little keep-at-home-and-out-of-sight gal that boosts his ego when he needs it. Marriage is not part of his latest plot. He's no better than a drugstore cowboy schmoozing with whoever can get him the next contract." She softened her tone. "I'm not saying he doesn't care for you. I'm saying you can't further his career. And until you can, Ross will always be his own first priority, and you will always come second. Or third. Or fourth."

"One day when I'm wearing a ring on this finger," she said, waving her left hand at Sally, "you'll tell me how happy you are for me. Then I'll remind you of this conversation."

"God love the meek and gullible," her friend responded with a shake of her head. "You have my number in Nevada. The phone is already disconnected at our apartment, so I'll drop you a line when George and I get back to LA. In the meantime, call Ruth if you need anything. She'll be able to find me."

"Yes, mother hen."

As Sally turned the old jalopy that George's friend had loaned them down Ivy Lane, an irritated *me-oow* sounded from the backseat. "Oh, poor Punkinhead. You've been such a good girl through the whole trip," she purred back to the cat, playing with her paw as it pushed out of a hole in the cardboard box. "We're almost there. Almost home."

Home. Why had she said that? This place was unlike anything she had experienced in her life. Growing up in Chicago, the family had had no reason to venture out to the suburbs. Everything one needed was right in the city. Los Angeles had been no different, except warm with no miserable winters. This little town wasn't as big as some of the neighborhoods she'd visited.

The street wove around the outskirts, a tree or two rising protectively near each house, stretching to the end of the town. The knot in Eloise's stomach began to unravel. A dog barked inside a fence, another trotted along the road. She heard children playing in the distance. A peace settled over her, an inexplicable sense of belonging and contentment.

"There it is," she yelled in her excitement. "On the left, stop. There it is." Her hand was on the door before the car was in park. She pulled the seat forward and grabbed the cat box from the back. Sally pulled her suitcase from the trunk.

"You sound like the little girl from *Miracle on 34th Street*," she yelled back. "Hey, I'm not carrying all this by myself. Be careful, those steps might be rotten."

Eloise took in the old house. More of a cottage, really. It had a second floor with two windows. A faded blue shutter hung perilously by one hinge. Below the porch roof, the steps leading into the house sagged in the middle, appearing to smile at her. She grinned back. "I love it."

"You haven't even been inside. I'm betting after some strong coffee and sleep, you'll hightail it back to LA as fast as you can." She tested the first step, and then the second, before putting her weight down and opening the screen door.

The girls walked into the dark house, shadows of covered furniture rising like small ghosts to greet them. Sally dropped the suitcase, walked over to a heavy drape, and yanked it open. Dust flew from the material, spiraling in the rays of light that poked through the dirty picture window. Eloise sneezed, and Punkinhead let out a high-pitched growl. She opened up the box, and the cat peeked out, a glint of light shining over her orange spot, giving the impression of a cartoon halo.

The tiny living room held a chair, an end table, and a sofa long enough to lie down on. It was a plain brown material, worn at the corner seams but in decent condition. The yellowed wallpaper, covered with faded roses and ivy, peeled from beneath the crown molding. Everything needed a good beating.

"Let's get your stuff out of the trunk," Sally said as she wiped her hands on her jeans. "Then we'll see if the rest of the house is as bad."

After carrying in her few meager boxes and their recent purchases, they investigated the kitchen. Large and spacious, it looked out to the backyard, the desert, and the mountain range beyond.

A table with rusted legs and matching chairs sat in the middle of this room. Dust covered the counters and cupboards next to the icebox; a stove and sink stood against the opposite wall. Pulling back the skirt below the sink, she saw a few pots and pans. She found some plates and glasses inside a cabinet and a drawer that held utensils and some silverware.

The back door led out to a well-kept yard where Punkin-head promptly began scratching her back against the bottom step. "That's nice. Whoever the agency hired has done a good job. Go ahead and investigate but don't go far," she told her pet. "You're all I've got once she leaves."

Sally threw an arm around her shoulder. "We'll see each other again soon. And I have to tell you. I'm not crazy about this work he's put on you, but I bet the sunsets here are swell. You're surrounded by mountains on all four sides." She gave a low whistle. "And the breeze. With the heat coming off the Mojave Desert, you'll appreciate that."

The bedroom was off the living room and held a full-size bed with a matching dresser. The closet had a wooden pole running across the back and a shelf above that ran the length of the space. Upstairs was a dormer filled with boxes from the previous owner. "I think I'll save these for a rainy day," she said, poking one with her toe.

"You aren't in Chicago anymore, honey. This is the desert —only a true procrastinator waits for rain." Sally laughed. "There might be some treasures hidden away up here. Ya never know."

An hour later, the old Chevrolet faded into the dust, and Eloise felt strangely calm. Her friend's words replayed in her head.

"Stay to yourself. People in these small towns like to gossip, and you'll be perfect fodder for the old geezers." They had hugged each other one more time. "Besides, you might end up actually liking the place, and then I'll never see you again."

All alone, she beamed as she looked back up at the house and tied a handkerchief on her head, tucking her shoulder-length hair behind her ears. The cat rubbed at her ankle, asking for attention. "I've got a good feeling about this place, Punkin. I can't quite put my finger on it but…"

She scratched at the black and brown fur and wondered why this place gave her such a sense of belonging. It pulled her in with visions of a porch swing, children running in the yard, a hope for the future. No, she wouldn't be running back to Los Angeles anytime soon.

After several hours of cleaning, dusting, and putting away her few boxes, Eloise decided it was time for lunch. She fixed herself a sandwich, grabbed a Seven-Up, and headed out to the front steps. Satisfaction filled her as she thought of her accomplishments so far. The living room and kitchen were habitable, and the bedroom closet was cleaned out with her clothes put away. The sheets were airing out on the line in the back.

"Good afternoon," a deep voice said, making her jump and the soda fizz and spill out of the bottle top. "I'm sorry, miss. I didn't mean to scare you."

"It's all right, I just—" The darkest pair of brown eyes she had ever seen stared at her with a friendly smile. "I'm... uh..."

Punkinhead came running around the side of the house, a big hound dog in pursuit. She lunged at Eloise, clinging to her shoulders with her claws as the canine barked and wagged its tail, long ears flapping back and forth.

"Ouch!" She stood up, trying to peel the nails from her shirt and kicking at the jumping dog. "Go away, stop it."

A large, calloused hand grabbed the leather collar and pulled the dog back. "Sit, Gus," he said with authority. "Good boy." Then he carefully lifted the cat's paws from her shirt, cradled the feline against his chest, and bent toward the dog.

"What are you doing? He'll tear her apart."

But Gus sniffed tentatively, his tail thumping the ground. A long tongue trailed up the cat's face, and then all went quiet. She stared in amazement at the mail carrier. His short, dark hair gleamed in the sun under his cap, and those coffee eyes smiling at her in amusement seemed familiar. The mailman and two critters made a hilarious picture, and laughter bubbled out of her until she bent over, clutching her stomach. His deep chuckle soon joined hers, along with the happy barking of Gus.

"Hello," the stranger finally said when she caught her breath. "I'm Victor Burnham, the Ridgecrest postman."

"Hi, I'm Eloise Kolby. You have quite a way with animals," she answered as she reached for her cat. "And this is Punkinhead."

"Let me guess. It has something to do with that orange spot." He rubbed the top of the cat's head. "Quite an original name. I bet you get looks when you have to call for her."

She giggled, immediately liking this tall, handsome man. He had a weathered look to him, as if he were outside most of the time. Not the groomed tan of Hollywood, achieved through tennis games a few hours at a time, but a darker, more permanent color. He smiled, showing straight white teeth, and the deep lines that creased his cheeks made her stomach flip just a little.

"So you're the mystery owner? The town has been wondering when you'd show up since Harry got a call to get the house opened." He squinted against a ray of light that poked through the old pine. "Where are you from?"

Sally's words of warning came rushing back to her. "Oh, by the coast. My, uh, fiancé inherited the place, and I've come to investigate." That wasn't giving away too much. "Harry?"

"Harry works for the appliance store and is the local handyman. If it's broken, he can fix it."

"I see. Then I assume everything is in working order." Her friend had been right about small towns and knowing everyone's business.

"Don't know. That would be between him and whoever wrote the check." He reached down and scratched Gus behind the ears. "Are you planning on selling?"

"Depends." Now what had she gotten herself into? She

was suddenly engaged. Next, her imaginary family would be moving into town. *Thanks, Sally.*

"Depends on what?" Victor sat down on the steps as if he were a familiar visitor. He studied her face intently. "It needs a bit of work."

"I noticed." Eloise suddenly wondered what she looked like after hours of cleaning. "It took most of the morning just to make the living room and kitchen decent for habitation."

"I can tell." The amusement in his eyes contradicted his serious face. "Well, I'll be happy to write down some names of folks who can help you out while you're here."

"Help me out?" The thought of a horde of strangers converging on her little private heaven didn't appeal to her. "I think I'm fine."

"Well, you'll need someone to check the roof, make sure the fuse box is up to snuff, and check the windows and doors before the next sand storm. Did you find much sand when you swept?" He waited patiently for a reply.

"Well, yes, but I assumed it was from years of—"

"Neglect. And I don't know if Mrs. Jenkins sent out her laundry because she didn't have a washing machine or just couldn't manage by herself. You might want to check the shed." He nodded toward the back of the house. "I'll be happy to give you a list of names of who does what around here when I come by on Monday."

"Thank you. That's very kind." He was, she realized. It showed in his face. Not only kind but gentle. A part of her wanted to reach out and touch his arm, let him know how much she appreciated his thoughtfulness.

"Until Monday then." He tipped his hat, the black bill glinting from the sun, then whistled. Gus came trotting from around the house. The dog followed him out the gate. To her surprise, Punkin tried to do the same.

Eloise scooped up the striped traitor and went back into

the house. Passing a mirror, she gasped. She stared at the reflection, wiping at the thin film of dust and dirt that covered her scarf, face, and neck. One clean swipe down her left cheek noted where the cat had placed her paw during the trauma.

"And the man managed to keep a straight face. Now, let's hope the tub works, and I don't need rescuing from the plumber!"

CHAPTER 5

*V*ictor couldn't decide if fate smiled down at him today or just toyed with him. Eloise—such a lovely name, lovelier girl—even with a dirty raccoon face. He'd recognized her immediately from that long-ago day in LA. She'd been a breath of fresh air in a city of smog.

He hadn't known for certain if the house had somehow been sold from under him until he met her. The fiancé talk didn't fool him. A man didn't propose to a woman without giving her a ring. A good man, anyway. They had no definite plans of moving in, so it seemed that his time had come.

All of Ridgecrest knew that house belonged to him. Everyone was just waiting for the legalities. He figured by next year, he would have two lawns to maintain. His mother's house and Ivy Lane. He'd taken over the upkeep of his childhood home after his father's death last year. Pop had gone quick. Smiling one moment, on the floor of the high school gym the next. He had been working one evening, cleaning up after a dance. Some teenagers had stopped back in and found him on the floor. The doc said he'd gone just like that, snapping his fingers. Nevertheless, they'd taken him to Drummond Hospital to make it official.

Victor didn't know what was worse, watching someone die slowly like his uncle with cancer, or losing them suddenly like his dad. Either way was full of pain and made him think long and hard about life. Every day counted, he told himself. Even the bad ones.

The beauty who now occupied his future house had been an unexpected pleasure. When he'd looked into those clear, blue eyes, she'd taken his breath away again. His usual confident manner had fled. Gus saved the day and gave him a reason to let himself into the yard. She wasn't much of a talker, though.

Walking into Tiny's, he sidled up to the short counter that might fit all of three people, depending on their size. "Hiya, Mary. Can I get a cheeseburger, add mayo and onion?"

"Anything for my favorite mailman," she called over the sizzle of the grill. "Take a seat before we get packed. School will let out soon, and it will be standing room only."

"Good idea. How about a strawberry shake too?"

"Tiny—burger with cheese, onion, and mayo. I'm headed out front." The plump, dark-haired woman pushed her short waves behind her ears and came around to the counter. Scooping ice cream into the silver cup, she squirted in strawberry syrup and grinned over her shoulder. "Coming from Ivy Lane?"

"You must be a mind reader. How did you know?"

The buzz of the mixer stopped the conversation for a moment. Then she spooned the creamy mixture into the soda glass.

"It's almost three o'clock, and you always come by at this time. Ivy is the last street on your route." Mary plopped the shake in front of him, reached under the counter, and pulled out a spoon and straw. With the edge of her apron, she wiped off the spot of pink that had dripped off the edge of the glass onto the counter. "Did you see her? What's she look like?"

"Who?" Victor grinned at the impatient look. "Bobby at the station was right. The redhead is gone, and the blonde is still here. Her name is Eloise, and she seems very nice."

"How long did you talk to her?"

He shrugged. "Fifteen minutes. Gus gave me an excuse to go into the yard. He wanted to play with her cat."

"Aw, poor Gus. He misses his buddy, Tabby."

"She thinks I'm a miracle worker and saved her cat from certain death," he added with a wink. "We won't tell her any different, will we?"

"Your secret is safe with me." The clatter of a plate at the window made them look up.

"So is she single? Is she moving in?" Tiny bellowed across from the kitchen. "That'll cramp your plans. You'll have to court her first, then you'll get the house *and* the girl."

"Her name is Eloise, no ring, though she says she's engaged, and you can ask her yourself. I'm sure she'll be around," Victor yelled back with a grin. "I'll add your name to the list of helpful people I'm making for her."

"Wise guy. Give me that burger back, Mary. I need to add some humble pie to it."

Victor wrote on his napkin with an imaginary pencil. "Tiny, matchmaker with no finesse."

"I hate to say this," Mary contradicted, "but in his day, my husband had plenty of finesse."

"That's right," he agreed loudly. "How ya think I got that gem?" He blew a kiss to his wife and scraped the grill clean.

Mary patted Victor's arm. "Things will work out the way they're supposed to. They always do. Just know we're rooting for you."

* * *

MONDAY DAWNED BRIGHT AND HOPEFUL. Victor entered the post office, singing an old tune from the war. "Mairzy doats and dozy doats and liddle lamzy divey. A kiddley divey too, wouldn't you?"

The postmaster grinned. "I haven't heard that one in years. What made you think of it?"

"Don't know. Just popped into my head. One of those songs you want to remember to sing to your kids and hear 'em laugh." Victor stopped. *Why are kids on my mind?*

His dreams last night had been odd too. A girl with a blonde ponytail swinging under the pine tree in his back-yard, a little boy with dark hair toddling around the front, lugging an unwilling cat. With a big orange spot on its head. *Doesn't that take the cake?* he thought. *An ordinary Joe having dreams about a Rodeo Drive gal.*

He went to the back and grabbed the big canvas bag. "Neither snow nor rain, nor heat nor gloom." Victor put a hand to the side of his mouth and continued, "and in Califor-nia, nor earthquakes nor sandstorms—"

"Nor beautiful blondes, stays these couriers from the swift completion of their appointed rounds." The older man chuckled. "Now go see what you can find out about our Mystery Woman at 19 Ivy Lane."

That afternoon, Victor wiped the sweat from his forehead and stuffed the handkerchief back in his bag. The yard looked empty from here, but as he got closer, the door opened and out stepped Eloise. She walked to the mailbox and waited, an envelope in her hand.

"Good afternoon, miss." He gave a royal bow and then held out his hand for the letter. "Or will you forever remain 'The Mystery Woman' to the town of Ridgecrest?"

She laughed. A delightful, pure sound that floated over him like a wispy cloud on a perfect day. Then those eyes were on him, those blue eyes the color of a cornflower. He had to untie his tongue before he could speak again.

"They don't really call me that, do they?"

Her blush gave color to her pale skin, and he found himself wanting to brush the back of his fingers across her cheek. For the first time in his life, he was not comfortable with a woman. His easy manner and good looks attracted most of the available females in the area. Yet, no one affected him like this doll from... Chicago! Yes, she'd come from the Windy City if he remembered correctly.

"Yes, they do. It doesn't take much to stir up this little town." To his relief, the words flowed again, and he relaxed. "Let me be the hero of the town and fill them in on the big secret."

"I'm a spy, and the communists are coming to take over the desert. They heard about the treasure that was buried here by the Ridgecrest founder." She paused and looked both ways. "But I sneak out each evening with Special Agent Punkinhead, hoping to find it before they do."

"Then you'll use it to trap them and save California." He smacked himself on the forehead. "Of course, I should have thought of that."

"Now that my secret is out, here is a very coded message." She handed him the envelope. "I'm not sure about the postage. I've never sent anything overseas before."

"Rome, eh?"

"Yes, my fiancé is there on location shooting a film." Her pride was obvious as she spoke.

"An actor, then?"

"No, a screenwriter," she answered. "He's hoping this is his big break. I'm hoping too."

"Then he'd come back, and you'd both settle here?" He shook his head. "What will the folks think about show business folks moving in?"

"Oh, Ross would never... He prefers..."

"More the big city type?"

She nodded, turning her head quickly. He'd seen the tears shining in them as she pretended to look for her cat.

"Here's what I'll do. I'll take care of this delivery for you today, and you can pay me tomorrow. Sound good?"

He watched the back of her head nod.

"And I have that list for you."

She turned back around, eyes red but dry now. "Thank you so much. I'm not sure how long I'll be here, so I should get everything inspected."

"I'll see you tomorrow then."

* * *

The next month, the two of them established a routine. The highlight of his day became the Ivy Lane visits. Each day, she met him at the mailbox with a letter. It was always addressed to either Ross Wilson in Rome, Sally Berkeley in LA, or Pauline Kirby in Chicago. Each day, he learned just a little more about her. Eloise had come from a big family in Chicago. He gathered her father was not close to his children, with a stepmother she'd never become acquainted with. Not that Eloise ever made a derogatory remark against either of them. It was what she didn't say. She spoke of her siblings and mother who had passed with great affection.

Every night now, while he lay in bed, he tried to think of a joke or story that would make her laugh. It was a sound he looked forward to, and thinking of her helped him sleep. She was becoming part of his life with these brief daily encounters. It excited and scared the hell out of him.

The folks around town called her Hollywood after

finding out her fiancé was a big screenwriter. Eloise was the closest they had ever been to Gregory Peck and Audrey Hepburn, or any other star for that matter. No one cared Eloise hadn't met either of them. She was *associated* through her fiancé.

Her silk headscarf and sunglasses had become a signature look with the high school girls too. Eloise only laughed and shook her head when she saw a group of them walking and giggling together.

It had taken her two weeks to enter Shoaf's Café. The bell above the door tinkled, and there she stood with the light at her back, a shadowed outline of scarf and skirt. The place went silent.

He recognized her hesitation, that instinct to run, and was at her side before she could flee. By the time the lunch special arrived, at least a dozen people had stopped to introduce themselves and welcome her to the town. The pleasure on her face had been unmistakable.

"She's not used to such attention," Rita said one day, setting down a pastrami sandwich and potato salad. "You'd think a looker like that would be accustomed to people staring."

"I'm still figuring her out myself."

"Just be careful, Victor. Miss Kolby is a nice lady, but she's engaged."

Does it show? Am I that transparent ,or do they know me that well?

"This is the first gal you've pinned with those big brown eyes and see nothing else in the room," she said matter-of-factly. "Your mama's been waiting to see that look for a long time. Has she met her yet?"

His mother lived in the nearby town of Inyokern. He went to see her every Sunday since his father died, more often if he could get away. Mom was coping well with a community of support helping them along. In a crisis, the residents of Ridgecrest bound together like family.

"Mom's due to come into town next week to meet up with you fine ladies, isn't she? Maybe we'll arrange a meeting then," he said carefully. "I'm sure news of the Mystery Woman has reached Inyokern, so she'll be curious."

"I don't know if that's the word I'd use, but Martha will certainly want to meet this one."

* * *

ELOISE SAT in her living room on the old brown sofa, waving the paper in front of her face. The electric fan whirred but only seemed to stir the heavy air. Heat had never bothered her, but then again, she'd never lived in the desert. The windstorms had taken time to get used to. They were frequent but not harmful if you stayed inside. Once, she tried to call Punkin from the porch and ended up with a wind and sand burn on her legs. It stung but had no lasting effects. After that, when the wind picked up, she found her cat right away.

The house was presentable and ready to put on the market. No reason to decorate if Ross didn't want to live here, but her mind would drift to what the place would look like if she could do what she wanted. The wallpaper would go, and lightweight, colorful drapes would hang in every room. The kitchen needed paint. A bright, cheerful yellow with white cabinets. The woodwork could be stripped again and bring out the light oak.

She loved this house. When Eloise thought of married life and happiness, the image of a house just like this popped into her head. Yes, this home begged for some love and attention. She didn't really need a phone and could use some of the money in Ross's account to fix it up a bit more. After all, it could only improve the value. And if she might be here six months… Maybe she should get a job. Make some friends.

Ross had not yet written. He had been gone a month and could have at least dropped her a postcard. Was he even opening her letters? Or reading them with that actress and laughing together? She knew thoughts like that weren't fair. He could be truly busy, making a name for himself, for them. Besides, men didn't like to write anyway. Except that he *was* a writer.

Then there was Victor, her saving grace over the past few weeks. When she finally found the courage to have lunch in town, the customers in the little diner had gawked at her collectively. She wasn't a star, didn't even know any. Being on the same movie set, but never the same day, was as close as she'd ever come. Yet she seemed to be an enigma to the folks of Ridgecrest.

One of nine children with a father who barely remembered her name, she didn't know how to act when all eyes were on her. Even on set, she was always one of many. That day, Victor had come to her rescue again. First with Punkinhead, and then at Shoaf's. Is that the only way she could meet a man? As a damsel in distress?

Eloise had been grateful to him. He had sensed she wanted to turn and run, not caring if it started more rumors. Then he was there, an arm around her shoulders, pulling her into a booth. The whole place had suddenly wanted to meet her.

She found it interesting how he had traits similar to Ross: an easygoing manner, the ability to pull someone from their shell, and a handsome face. Yet, there were significant differences. Ross socialized to get something from a person. Victor enjoyed people, just plain liked them. And they liked him. It showed in every face that crossed his way, including her own.

Guilt flooded her at the thought of comparing the two men. Sally would clap with glee, but she was ashamed by her lack of loyalty. Ross was a different type of man, and she had known that from the beginning. She'd come to recognize his need for someone to help *him* shine. Deep down, she had known that and enjoyed the warmth of his light, enjoyed the attention of being his main girl. No, her personality didn't fit into the Hollywood scene. On Ross's arm, Eloise could be important without the pressure of fame. The background role suited her.

Main girl. Perhaps. Truthfully, she wasn't sure anymore. Since arriving here, Eloise began to wonder why she settled for being his "best" girl. Why did she hang on in this place, waiting for that letter?

Chase that dream and have no regrets.

When had that dream truly turned from Hollywood into love and marriage? The thought gave her a jolt. It was unsettling to recognize how imperceptible the change had occurred.

She looked at her watch. Almost 2:30. Guilt niggled at her as she took a quick glance in the mirror. She had decided to only write once a week instead of every other day, rationalizing that it would save money that could be put into the house. Her daily chats with Victor continued without a comment from either of them about the decrease in correspondence. As she walked out to the mailbox, he came toward her, unhurried, a slow smile across his face. Her eyes took in the tall, muscular form in the dark uniform. The material of his cotton shirt strained as he reached back to pull a package from his bag. An image popped into her mind of him on the beach, his bare chest wet and gleaming…

Oh my! Where did that come from?

"Good afternoon, Miss Kolby. I regret I have no mail for you today." Cap off, he bowed low. "Is there anything I can do for you?"

"Why, Mr. Burnham, if you are sincere in your offer." Eloise giggled, feeling like a grade school girl, a blush spreading up her neck as she pushed away unbidden thoughts. "I'm in dire need of a job."

"Employment? So, you're thinking of settling in our little town? Did you receive a telegraph, or are you cheating on me with the postmaster and sneaking to the post box for secret correspondence?" He wiggled his dark eyebrows. "He's a bit long in the tooth, but I remain nonjudgmental."

With a loud sigh and a slump of her shoulders, Eloise quit the role-play. "If I stay here and wait, I need something to do. I can't stand it. Plus, you said there's talk of putting up an antenna. I may buy a television."

"Let me see what I can do. What experience do you have besides being a star?" The humor in his eyes refused to let her be indignant.

"Well, if there are no leading roles to be had… I've waitressed, been a receptionist—"

"You can answer a telephone?"

"Yes, I seem to do it rather well, even if I don't happen to have one here." She shrugged. "If I start earning a paycheck, that will change too."

"Last I heard, Melanie over at the switchboard was having a baby, so they may be short. Her husband wanted her to quit earlier, but she insisted on getting a new crib." He crossed his arms and looked at her. "Are you dependable and courteous?"

"Of course."

"Able to hold your irritation when Mrs. Davis calls you thirteen times asking for the same number, and then blames you for disconnecting her?"

"Oh my, she doesn't."

"I'm afraid so." His head nodded sadly. "Much to her son's dismay when she calls each week, says 'hello' thirteen times, then the line goes dead. Fourteen seems to be her lucky number."

"I'd love to deal with Mrs. Davis. Really." She looked down, choosing her words carefully. "I have never *not* worked. I need to feel useful, and waiting is not useful. Does that make any sense?"

"Absolutely. You don't need me really, but I'd be glad to escort you to the telephone office and introduce you." He smiled, reassuring her before any nervousness set in. "You may meet some new friends. I think it would be good for you."

She didn't want to admit she was lonely. Still uncomfortable venturing out alone, she longed for the camaraderie she saw in the diner and the market. Yes, everyone knew everyone's business. However, they also checked up on one another and cared for each other. If something weighed heavily on one's shoulders, there were people lined up to help with that burden.

Eloise thought that must be what a close family would be like. Driving her crazy and loving her unconditionally. Knowing by a look or an action that something was wrong or wonderfully right. As her mother had always been able to do.

Sharing each step of one's life with others, joyous or sad, was a gift. Oh, how she wanted that gift and didn't care if it came wrapped with a bow or in a paper sack. Then Victor said the sweetest she'd ever heard.

"By the way, a group of us are going to Inyokern Saturday night to watch some drag racing. Would you like to come?"

CHAPTER 6

$\mathcal{V}$ictor warned her of the noise before the roar of engines blasted their eardrums.

"This is worse than standing under the L train in Chicago," she yelled over the reverberation. "Only much more exciting."

Two cars, side by side, waited for the green flag. A quarter mile down the sandy road stood another man with a checkered flag.

"Who are you cheering for?" Eloise asked, her eyes on the souped-up red Chevy and the black Thunderbird.

"You mean who am I betting on?" Victor smiled and nodded his head. "If the T-Bird wins, I'm taking you out for dinner."

"And if the Chevy wins?"

"I'll cook. You eat at your own risk," he added with a wink.

"So, this is the airport? Drag racing is illegal in LA. I'm surprised to see the race at such a public place. Can we get in trouble?"

"If we get caught." At her wary look, he explained, "No one bothers us out here. There aren't many activities in the more rural areas, and as long as there's no trouble—or injuries—the chief turns his head. He was, by the way, an undefeated champion himself before he entered law enforcement."

"That's convenient. And lucky for us. Oh, they're getting ready!"

He noticed Eloise had been surprised at how many people attended an informal race like this. The enthusiasm and good-natured vibes back and forth between sides had all been in fun.

"But don't be fooled. Some races get very heated and competitive," he warned. "The Burroughs High boys are just fooling around and learning as they go."

Tonight, the group of high school boys tested out a couple of new hot rods. The green flag went down, tires spun, and a cloud of sand hovered over the crowd. He watched Eloise jump up and down, screaming for the T-Bird as it crossed the finish line under the checkered flag. Turning to him, she threw her hands around his neck and yelled, "We won, we won!"

Victor's arms went around her without thought. He watched the color spread across her cheeks as she realized what she had done and attempted to pull back. He didn't let go. Darned if his brain didn't tell him to release her, but his body had a mind of its own. So now what?

"I believe you owe me dinner," she said, the huskiness in her voice stirring his blood and other parts of his anatomy.

"Indeed, I do," he answered, his hold on her not budging as he looked down into those sky-blue eyes. "But right now, my stomach is the least of my worries."

Her face, infused with scarlet, made him inwardly curse

himself for his boldness. Then she surprised him. She leaned up on her tiptoes, brushing the length of his body, and whispered, "I know."

"Hey, lovebirds, come collect your winnings!" someone yelled from a distance. At least, it seemed like it came from far away as they stood there in their own little world.

"I think I need some help if I'm to remain a gentleman." He heard his own raw tone and hoped it didn't frighten her. The answering grin reassured him. He let go of her, his fingers trailing her waist and hips, then grabbed her hand, and ran toward the finish line.

"I hope it's enough for steak at the Homestead. First round is on me." A cheer went up.

"Who's up for a steak and a soda?" called out another girl, clinging to a tall, good-looking blond. A chorus of assent echoed through the dusty haze. "We'll meet there in twenty."

The guys divvied up the winnings. "Yeah, Vic is always lucky," mumbled one of the losers. "I wish I had his picker."

The driver of the T-Bird looked over his shoulder at Eloise and agreed with a whistle. "Yeah, me too."

Everyone got into their cars and headed to Inyokern. Silence sat between them as he backed up his copper-colored 1948 Chevy Fleetline. The rumble of the engine filled the cab, and the few feet between them seemed like miles. His hand itched to reach over, grab her tiny waist, and pull her against him. Tight. And kiss her until she gasped for air.

"So you're also called Vic?"

"Uh, yeah. By family and old friends." He glanced sideways to find her looking at him thoughtfully. "Do you have a nickname?"

"Elli. Except for my dad, who could never keep our names straight, my family and Sally call me Elli."

"What about Hollywood Man?" His eyes squinted for a

moment as he cursed himself for the second time that night. "I'm sorry. I had no right to say that."

"It's fine. He's never been a nickname kind of guy. More of a 'baby doll' and 'gal' type." She smoothed out her cotton slacks, and he watched the shapely muscle of her thigh through the material. "May I call you Vic?"

"Sure, if I can call you Elli."

"Deal!" She sounded happy, and he slowed the car down as he took a curve. "So tell me something else about your family. You seem to know a lot more about me than I do of you. You're very good at getting people to open up."

"That's why the town folk like me as the mailman. I find out all the good stuff."

She laughed. "I bet you do. Are your parents nearby?"

He carefully arranged his face. "My mother lives here in Inyokern. My father died of a heart attack about a year ago."

"Oh, I'm sorry. I shouldn't have…"

"Of course you should ask. No one reads minds, so how would you know? We were comforted by the fact that he went quickly with no pain," he told her, hoping to ease her mind. "In fact, we were in LA a couple of years ago to see a heart specialist. I went to a diner nearby… Have you ever worked at Harvey's diner?"

Her mouth fell open. "Yes! You came in there, didn't you? I knew your eyes seemed familiar. And you remember me?" Elli shook her head.

"Small world, isn't it?" He nodded, glad she had remembered him too.

"Do you have any brothers or sisters?" she asked, turning slightly in the seat to face him more directly.

"My little brother joined the service as soon as he turned eighteen. He's a pilot now, doing a stint over in Korea."

"Sally's husband just got back from Korea. He's a doctor. Well, a military doctor."

"The one who sent the postcards? Sally, the infamous redhead who had poor Bobby shaking in his boots? She made quite an impression in Ridgecrest."

"She makes quite an impression everywhere she goes." Eloise laughed. She told Victor how they met and how she brought her to Ivy Lane. "I miss her something awful."

"What else do you miss, Elli? Is the small town life making you stir crazy?"

"No, actually. It's growing on me. I don't think I realized quite how artificial Hollywood was until I came here." She paused, as if choosing her words. "The people here are so… genuine. It's as if everyone has their place and fits in."

"Do you mind if I ask how old you are?"

"Old enough, mister. What's on your mind?"

Victor chuckled at her Mae West imitation. "I'm guessing around twenty from our conversations. Am I close?"

"Very good. I left for LA on my eighteenth birthday, and I lived there two years. And you?"

Lights flashed ahead as several cars turned into a parking lot. The restaurant sat on the left, a long white building with arches covering a narrow patio entrance. Victor offered his arm as they walked through the parking lot.

"You didn't answer my question. How old are you?"

"Ancient." Would she consider him too old? Worry poked at him, but he couldn't be any older than Hollywood Man.

"And that would be?"

"Twenty-seven years young." Her silence unnerved him, and he kept his eyes ahead.

"Oh my, you must be considering retirement soon." She reached up and touched the hair above his ears, the back of her fingers stroking it softly. "And all the gray. Dear, dear."

"Gray? Why, I oughtta—"

She dashed away and ran into the Homestead ahead of him. Once inside, he saw her waiting by the bar, her full lips turned up at the corners. He tickled her sides. "You're a little minx."

The laugh washed over him like balm on a bee sting. His hand naturally went to her lower back as they joined the group in the far room. Several tables had been pushed together to accommodate the large number.

Her sense of humor and relaxed conversation surprised him as the evening progressed. Eloise listened to tales of local legends, ghosts, and growing up in the desert. Reciprocating, she described Chicago and the movie sets of MGM. Most of them had never been farther than Bakersfield, and Elli seemed such a refined woman to them.

Victor had caught the insecurity and hesitation in her eyes the first time they'd met in Ridgecrest. A warm feeling grew in his stomach as he realized she had grown comfortable with him and with the town residents. Deep down, she wanted to be a small-town girl herself. The trick was to get her to admit it.

* * *

Eloise stood inside the screen door as Victor walked away into the shadows. Her body screamed for his touch; her lips ached for his kiss. She knew he felt the same but had remained a gentleman with only a peck on her forehead and a promise to call. Now, how would he do that when she didn't have a phone?

Funny, the guilt no longer plagued her after waiting so long for a letter from Rome. Still, she appreciated the fact Victor didn't put her in an awkward position. His presence had become her one constant in the short time she had been in Ridgecrest. Had it really been over a month since she'd arrived? That would be... thirty days minus four Sundays: twenty-six mailbox rendezvous, one lunch at Shoaf's, and a drag race with dinner. Yet, she understood him better than she had ever understood Ross.

Monday, she started her new job at the telephone office. It had taken only a word from Mr. Burnham. They'd stopped by on their way to the airport, and Mr. Whitten had hired her on the spot. The lights and plugs, the girls with earphones and little speakers fascinated her. The switchboard position might turn into something long-term.

Her breath caught. The word *permanent* entered her brain. She was waiting for Ross Wilson, waiting to rejoin civilization and restart her career, not settling into small town desert life. So why did the thought of leaving this place make her feel empty inside? Sally would know what to do. She always had a plan.

A soft purr came from behind. Punkin, curled up on a pillow, had most definitely settled in. It turned out Gus lived two houses down, and the two animals had become the best of friends. His previous feline friend had died of old age, and Gus had lost his zest for life and his appetite—wouldn't even chew on a beef bone, the widow had said. Until Punkinhead moved in.

A stray had tried to chase Punkin one day, and Gus's gentle demeanor turned ferocious. The poor dog didn't stand a chance against the big hound. He'd slunk away with a squeal, and Punkin had shown her appreciation with rubs and purrs along Gus's belly.

The protective behavior reminded her of Victor the day she'd gone into the café. Eloise had never had a champion in her life except Sally. He had an essence about him that affected anyone in his vicinity. His confidence enveloped her, providing a sense of security that she'd always hoped to find. With Ross, uncertainty always prevailed.

Monday found her sitting in front of a UFO. At first overwhelming, she decided to treat it like the Battleship game. The lights flickered, tones beeped. "Operator, how may I help you?" By midmorning, Eloise had picked up the machinations of the switchboard. Mr. Whitten, a kind, older gentleman with orange-gray hair, had explained the workings of the plugs with practiced patience. The other two girls working with her today seemed friendly and pleasant.

She could find only one negative aspect to the job. No mailbox. No Victor. It hadn't occurred to her that this job would interfere with their daily visits. Pushing the disappointment aside, Eloise listened to the number, pulled one plug, and inserted another, connecting the call. The afternoon kept her busy.

"Operator, how may I help you?"

"Is that a loaded question?"

"Excuse me, but—" The smile split across her face, and she checked her watch. Two-thirty. He'd also been thinking about their daily rendezvous. "Victor?"

"How many men call you in a day?"

The deep timbre of his voice made her heart pound. She felt like a silly schoolgirl whose crush had finally remembered her number. "I haven't kept count but at least a dozen. Though none are as *mature* as you."

"Hey, there. No name-calling... Elli."

He spoke her name in a low, husky tone, sending heat straight through her. She wiggled her toes and sighed. "I love how you say my name."

"Good, I plan on saying it a lot. Did you enjoy Saturday night?"

"Very much. And you?" *Except you didn't kiss me, and I tossed and turned for hours.*

"Enough to hope for a repeat. Say, they play old classic

movies every Wednesday night at the theater. Would you like to go?"

"What's playing?" *Not that it mattered.*

"Phantom of the Opera." She could hear the smile in his voice. "They play the spooky ones in October. If you get scared, just hold on to me. I'll protect you."

"Always the considerate Joe, eh? Sure, I'd love to go."

"Great. See you at seven."

* * *

They fell into a new routine over the next few months. A movie in the middle of the week. A date with dinner on Saturdays. Victor would stop by on Sunday before visiting his mother to fix a faucet or a stuck window.

He had fallen in love with her. In moments of honesty, he admitted he'd probably loved her since he peeled the cat claws from her blouse that first day. An easiness developed between them. Conversations moved between teasing, life dreams, and learning new things about each other.

Hollywood Man no longer entered the dialogue. An insignificant bug on the windshield. Victor figured that if the imbecile cared about Elli, he would contact her. It had been four months—heck, a new year now. Neither had mentioned that her correspondence had dwindled to a monthly update. All is fair in love and war, right? Well, if the man did ever send that letter, it would be war. Victor had big plans for 1953, and Hollywood Man was not part of them.

His mother had met Elli on Thanksgiving, and they hit it off right away. Mrs. Burnham had seen a young, vibrant girl, looking for love and acceptance, and had given her just that. She had invited them both back the following Sunday, resulting in dinner with his mom being added to their weekly routine. The two women would cook together, Elli now bringing a dish with her as well. She never interfered in the kitchen or overstepped her bounds, just asked how to help as she tied on an apron.

THE HOLIDAYS HAD BEEN emotional for all of them—the second one without Pops. Sally and her husband, George, came for a visit. He liked Red. They'd had a nice long talk before she left, and Victor received her full blessing. It had given him the determination he needed to move ahead.

Victor had proceeded carefully these last months. He didn't want Elli shying away because of guilt, so he took the old-fashioned courting approach. They grew closer without any major physical contact between them. He chuckled when he considered that promise he had made to himself. This would be a relationship based on mutual respect and real love, not just passion. He groaned. *And it's killing me.*

He hadn't kissed her lips, run his fingers through those thick blonde waves, or moved his hands along those delicious curves, or... Memories of that day she had thrown her arms around him haunted him every night, and he'd wake up in a sweat with a smile on his face. Each time he was close enough to breathe in her sweet scent, feel the warmth of her leg against his as they sat on the front steps or watched television on the couch, he deserved a medal of honor.

They played the cat-and-mouse game well together, flirting back and forth. Victor would put his arm around the back of the couch and let his fingers graze her bare shoulder. Lightly, gently. Elli would push her thigh against him as she stood to get them more drinks or wipe a drop of soda from his chin. He would bend over her to point out an insect in the yard, his mouth dangerously close to her neck, sending his warm breath down her collar. She would feed him a bite of meat she had baking in the oven, and his tongue would touch her fingers as she pulled them away. Their eyes spoke, teased, and pleaded with the other.

Yeah, he had big plans for 1953. The Friday night game was over, and the dance was about to begin.

$\mathcal{V}$ictor arrived at the post office on a Friday. It was almost the third week of January, and he was making plans for Valentine's Day. "Let's see what I've got to sort today. I'm ready for the weekend, Boss."

Silence. He looked up to see a miserable expression on the postmaster's face.

"What is it?" Panic gripped his throat, and no more words would come when he saw the letter in the old man's hand.

"This came for Miss Kolby. It's… Well, it's…"

Was Hollywood Man finally claiming his girl? His panic turned to resentment. *You can't have her. You don't deserve her. I'll fight you for her, you son of a—*

"Victor, do you want me to deliver it?"

The rage he felt must have shown on his face. He drew in a slow, deep breath, collected himself, and then shook his head.

"No. I'll take it," he said, his voice hoarse. It was Elli's day off. What would her reaction be? The panic returned, hitting him in the gut with a force that made him wince. *Why now? He was making plans for his future, their future.*

At 2:30, she stood by the mailbox wearing her navy swing coat and a knitted cap, placed jauntily on her head. He wanted to laugh. True, it was unseasonably cool, but a coat and hat? She waited for him, her sweet lips upturned and expectant. His heart twisted, and he mentally kept his hand from clutching his chest. As he closed the gap between them, her smile faded.

"What is it? Is your mother okay?" The concern in her voice shoved the knife a little deeper.

He shook his head and reached into his bag. Her eyes followed, a look of surprise on her face when she saw two letters between his fingers. She immediately recognized the airmail stamp and male handwriting. Elli shook her head and stepped back.

"It's from Italy," he said simply and saw the dread in her eyes. Taking a step forward, he pressed the envelope into her coat. She looked down with a blank stare.

"I'll leave you alone but know this: I'm not giving up on us." He moved closer and took her face in his gloved hands, wishing he could feel the softness of her skin. "I'll see you tomorrow night, okay?"

She nodded without moving. When Victor reached the end of the block, he turned to see Elli still standing in the same spot, staring down at the letter.

* * *

ELOISE WOKE IN THE MORNING, her eyes red from crying and lack of sleep. She had tossed and turned, images of Victor, then Ross, invading her dreams. The letter had read like a telegram, short and sweet. Well, maybe not so sweet.

Eloise,

I'll be home within the month. Meet me back in LA. I've phoned the landlord to let him know you're coming. The filming went great. Minelli agreed to look at my script.

Missed you,

Ross

FOR AN AUTHOR, he hadn't put much time in the only letter he had finally sent. *Missed you.* The only hint of affection. It hurt. No inquiries about her or the house. It was all about him. Yet, deep in her heart she had always known that about Ross. Had her longing for attention kept the blinders on? Or had it been Victor who'd taken them off? Didn't she at least owe Ross a chance?

No.

If he had mentioned their future, or written words of love, maybe. Eloise wanted to block it out from her mind and pretend she'd never received the letter. But they would have to talk eventually. She was living on his property.

I'll cross that bridge when I come to it. Call him in a month, after he has settled in, and arrange to meet him.

The house shouldn't be a problem. Ross wanted the cash and wouldn't care who bought it. She may need to find another place to live temporarily, depending on how well Ross took the news. *He'll move on quickly enough.*

With her decision made, Eloise put her old life from her mind. She had a date tonight with the most wonderful man she knew. A grin replaced her frown.

Sally will flip a wig, she thought and laughed out loud.

* * *

THAT AFTERNOON, the wind picked up, so Eloise called out the back door for Punkinhead. She had taken to lying in the garden, as if waiting for the spring flowers to begin their bloom. Victor had told her that Mrs. Jenkins had carefully tended the wildflowers and, of course, he'd kept them thriving.

She had seen little color since her arrival, the plants dormant during the drought season, but looked forward to the new buds in the coming months. Who would have thought a colorful garden might be possible in the Mojave? *A desert is an amazing place*, she thought as she wandered out to find her disobedient cat.

The sand began its dance along the street, swirling and swatting at anything in its way. A finger of dread poked at her as she hurried toward Gus's house.

"Punkin, Punkinhead," she called over the widow's gate. "Hi there, Gus. Where's your best friend?" The dog gave a friendly bark and wagged his tail, coming up to the fence and giving her hand a sloppy lick.

An elderly lady peeked out from the door. "You better get inside, honey. That wind is stronger than usual."

"Yes, ma'am. As soon as I find Punkin."

Eloise ran home and grabbed a scarf and glasses to protect her hair and eyes from the sand and bits of debris now blowing about. Standing on the edge of her property, she studied the desert plain for movement. The wind broke for just a second, and a tail whipped from under a black brush bush. Her silly cat hated these storms and thought she could hide under it. With a sigh, she weaved through the scrub and wild grasses.

As she drew closer, Eloise heard the frantic *meow* that signaled a frightened feline. She hurried to the bush, and Punkin all but jumped at her. The sunglasses flew into a dense patch of scrub. Clinging to the cat, she turned to run back to the house. The wind increased and in a flash, the visibility went to zero. The strength of the gale forced her to a kneeling position, and she crouched low, her head tucked against the soft fur of her cat. Fear wrapped around her, a sheer deadly net that held her as tightly as the sand.

Tiny pebbles pelted her skin and slid down her neck and into the tiniest openings. It collected under her collar, between her breasts, and inside her waistband. She felt sand pile around her shoes and knees. *Could I be buried alive?* Tumbleweeds bounced off her head and back and tore at her skin, pulling at the scarf that clung to her hair and chin.

Eloise tried to open her eyes in between gusts, but the sharp sting made her snap them shut. The grit scraped under her lids, and tears streamed down her face. The salty moisture pooled at the corners of her lips, allowing dust to seep inside her mouth.

I'm going to die out here. Oh God, I'm going to die without ever seeing my family or Sally again. Or Victor.

His face, watery and beautiful, shimmered before her. She reached out, sure it must be an angel, but a strong hand grabbed her fingers. "I've got you. It's okay, I've got you."

Sturdy arms enveloped her, and the wind broke for a moment. Victor wrapped himself around her like a tent, taking the force of the wind and holding her tight. "Just give me a minute to get my bearings again, sweetheart. You'll have to help me because I don't know how long this storm will last."

A silent nod was all she could manage. Her heart pounded, but the terror receded. If anyone could get them safely home, Victor could. "My glasses... fell off. I can't... see. Sorry." Eloise tried to yell above the howling wind, but her voice cracked again with fresh panic, and sand coated her tongue. Her throat was raw, and she couldn't swallow. The tears continued to burn her eyes and the cuts on her face.

He spoke into her ear. "Hush, now. We'll be home in no time. All you have to do is stay next to me." She felt him rearrange his body around her, then his grip loosened. "We have to go between the gusts. Each time I can see our house, we'll go forward until the visibility is low again, then wait for the next break. Ready?"

With a nod, Eloise tried to get off her knees, but her joints screamed in pain. She managed to stay upright, though still crouched low. Victor secured her to his side, his arm in a vice-like grip around her waist. They advanced only a few feet before he pushed on her back to signal her to go down.

Time became insignificant compared to the distance they could travel. Counting steps each time they moved forward, she rejoiced when they finally made it to ten. Each inch, each foot, her will grew stronger. In Victor's protective hold, she instinctively knew she was safe. He would not let anything happen to her.

"I'm going to pick you up next time. I think we're close enough that I can get inside the yard. The tree will give us a windbreak." His words bounced against her eardrum and faded into the storm. "Hold on to that cat, and I'll shelter you from falling debris."

The whining of the wind lessened, and her feet left the ground. She clung to Punkin and buried her head in his broad shoulder. A crack sounded from above, then a thud. Victor stumbled but did not fall. She felt his thighs lift up one at a time as he went up the two back steps, fumbled with the doorknob, and stepped into the kitchen. He set her down carefully in a chair. With a growl, Punkinhead leaped from her lap and disappeared under the couch.

"Don't move. I'll get some water and a washcloth." She heard steps cross the room, the faucet run, and water splashing. A rustling under the sink as the curtain was pulled back;

a cabinet door opened, followed by the clink of glass. The water ran again, then a swishing and spitting noise. "Ah, that's better. Now, sit still while I clean you. If you drink now, you'll get a mouthful of sand."

A cold cloth dampened her lips, then swathed her eyes. His other hand held her cheek and chin in his palm, and she instinctively leaned into it. Her knuckles moved toward her lids. "Don't," he said sternly. "Rubbing will scratch the cornea. Let me get the majority of the sand off first, then we'll irrigate."

"Thank—" The scratching in her throat sent her into a spasm of coughs, followed by a terrible burning sensation.

"*Shhh*. I know, it hurts."

She nodded, her eyes tearing up again and burning the tender lids.

"Take a sip of water, but don't drink it. Rinse out your mouth and spit it back into this glass. You don't want to swallow the sand. I have a second glass with clean water. Okay?"

Another silent nod. She just wanted to see him. Look at his dear face and thank him for… for being there. For being Victor. After a good rinse, she took a long drink. The fire in her throat lessened, and he took her by the elbow and led her to the sink.

"I have a bowl of water here. When you feel it near, put your face in it and open your eyes. Move them around in a circle so the water can get in and clean out the sand. It won't be pleasant at first." His tone was calm, as if he were giving directions to the bank. "How are you doing?"

"Good," she croaked. He chuckled with that deep, delicious sound she had grown to love. When the pain subsided, she held out a hand for a towel and wiped her face, smoothing back her wet hair.

Her eyes opened, and she gasped. "Oh no, Vic. What

happened?" Her fingers flew to the side of his neck, dried blood staining his collar. "Sit down, what hit you?"

"A tree branch, I think. Maybe a roof tile, I don't know. It's just a scratch." He sat down with a grin. "Go ahead, Doc. Your turn."

Eloise bent over him, looking at the gash and lump on the back of his head. It was hard for her eyes to focus and took several moments to see the extent of his wound. Whatever smacked him had gotten him good. "This could be a concussion. You need to see a doctor."

"NO!"

The forcefulness of the word made her flinch. "But—"

"No," he said in a quieter but adamant tone. "The only doctor is at Drummond Hospital. By the time the storm subsides, the swelling will be down."

It wasn't seeing a doctor that bothered him, she thought with certainty. It was going to the hospital where his father had been taken.

"You *are* human," she said softly. "I didn't think you were afraid of anything." Her fingers pushed back his disheveled hair, tracing around the back of his ear, then down his neck. "It's nice to know."

"I'm afraid of a lot of things." He grabbed her wrist and put his lips to her palm, his other hand pulling her between his legs. He drew her close, his breath tickling her face as he spoke. "I'm terrified of losing you."

The sincerity in his deep-brown eyes sent an ache through her chest. Heat flooded her cheeks as he pulled her head down, and his lips brushed hers. The fleeting touch stole her breath. She stood there, eyes closed, waiting. His mouth covered hers again, kneading and nibbling, asking for more. Strong fingers entwined in her hair while his thumbs stroked her cheeks, creating a slow burn deep inside her. Ross had never stoked a fire in her like this.

AUBREY WYNNE

When the kiss ended, they remained silent except for the hushed sound of panting. Their foreheads touched, and for a moment, Eloise thought she might dissolve into a puddle at his feet. It had been the type of kiss Gable gave Lombard or Tracy gave Hepburn. The type of kiss a girl always wanted but didn't really believe in.

"Are you okay?" His fingers pushed her hair behind her ear and lightly rubbed her arm. "It just kind of happened."

Elli nodded, her eyes streaming again as she wiped the wetness from her cheeks. "It was… perfect."

"No, I don't believe so." He pulled her onto his lap. "It's something we need to work on." And he kissed her again, this time more demanding. She felt him let go of his reserve, devouring her like a starved man. Her pulse raced, and heat scorched her core. How did her heart beat way down there? Then her mind went blank, and she surrendered to him, let him fill that secret chamber in her heart that had remained empty for so long.

* * *

IT TOOK two weeks for the scrapes and scratches to fully heal. Victor's head remained sore for a bit longer. He didn't mind. For the rest of his life, a sandstorm would bring a smile to his face. It had given him Elli. They saw each other every day now. If she wasn't at home during his route, he called her at the switchboard. Mr. Whitten, an old friend of Pop's, turned a blind eye to the brief personal phone calls.

When Victor had questioned her about the letter, she answered with a shake of her head. "Are you going back to Hollywood Man?" he'd asked quietly. Another shake of her soft, blonde waves. He had seen the pain in her eyes, sensed the rejection in her silence, and never brought it up again. It didn't matter because Elli was staying.

They continued the Wednesday, Saturday, and Sunday routine but shared a meal, soda, or bottle of beer every night at her place or his small apartment above the pharmacy. The temperatures had dropped, and February was hitting record lows. He'd been worried about her reaction to the cold, then remembered she'd been raised in Chicago.

Elli made him feel sixteen again. His pulse raced at the end of each day, knowing he would be with her, touching her, tasting those sweet, full lips. Valentine's Day was next week, and he had her present ready. It sat on his dresser, black velvet surrounding shining gold and a clear, sparkling stone. If only Ridgecrest and his mother could keep the secret. *I should have gone to Bakersfield to buy the ring.*

He headed over to Elli's house for a special dinner she had promised. She stood by the window, playing with the television. On a good day, the town might get two channels, but the heavy winds had knocked down the antenna put up by the naval station. There was talk of a new, improved antenna that would give them all the major networks. Victor worried it would take the excitement out of the whole adventure. If someone was able to get a clear picture, folks jumped, yelled, and called all their friends. A living room could fill up in under ten minutes, and the guests would stay until fuzz once again filled the screen.

"Let me entertain you, Hollywood."

She jumped but turned with a smile. "It's been a long time since I heard that moniker." She leaned up on tiptoes, her arms around his neck, and gave him a loud smack on the mouth.

"I think you can do better than that. Let's pretend it's a screen test." His voice went husky, and he pulled her against his chest. She leaned in for another kiss. When their lips met, one hand moved behind her neck and pulled her back in a low dip. He didn't let her up until the blood had rushed to his head.

"The part is yours," she said, breathless. "Oh, wait. It's my audition."

Victor took off his coat, thinking of the black box in his pocket. After a dream last night that he'd forgotten to bring it to the dance, he decided to carry it with him. He wasn't taking any chances.

"Vic, can I ask you a question?"

"Soitenly!"

"When you rescued me from the sandstorm, you made a comment about *our* house." Her eyes searched his. "You realize I don't own this home?"

"Yes."

"Then why would you say that?"

He gave a sigh and followed her into the kitchen. Leaning against the counter, hands folded across his chest, he tried to explain. "It's common knowledge around town that I've wanted to buy this house. I looked for that sign in the yard every day until you moved in. I've been volunteer caretaker of this place since Mrs. Jenkins died."

"Oh, I see. And a swell job you've done."

"I was worried when you first came to town, then realized my time had come. I figured I'd be in this house by spring."

"And what about me?" She chewed her bottom lip, staring at her toes.

"I'm hoping I can work you into the contract. It'd be a sweet deal."

Her shoulders began to shake. Had he upset her? Then came that lovely tinkle of laughter. "Holy moly, buyer requests all equipment in the shed, appliances, and lady in the kitchen."

"And the cat. We can't forget Punkin." Victor sniffed the air. "What's for dinner? You said something special?"

At first, he thought Elli had found out about the ring. His palms got sweaty when he pictured himself down on one knee, asking her to make him the happiest man in the county. He watched her stir something on the stove and wondered if this was how Pops had felt with Mom. He rarely remembered an argument between them. Pops had always said he would do anything for his wife.

Now Victor knew what he had meant. He would lay down his life for this woman, give up everything. A world without Elli would be bland and lackluster. She was the first thing he thought of when he opened his eyes and the last thing on his mind before he fell asleep. Sure, this would pass. But he knew the constancy of the emotion, the essence of his love for her, would never fade.

Elli chuckled. "I tried a new recipe for Valentine's Day. Heart-shaped meatloaf with Cupid potatoes mixed with beans and Red Velvet cake."

"Cupid potatoes? I'm nervous." He opened the oven and peeked inside. The smell made his mouth water. "You certainly can cook. I hope my present is equal to your dinner."

"You didn't get me a present. Oh!" She clapped her hands. "I never had many presents as a girl. It doesn't matter what it is. Anything from you, Mr. Burnham, will do nicely."

"Back to my question. What are Cupid potatoes?"

"Well, according to the cookbook, you add some red pepper to the potatoes and green beans for *zing*. The *zing* represents Cupid's arrow piercing his victim. Cute, huh?"

"Peachie." He swooped her up in his arms and carried her into the living room.

She kicked her legs in mock protest. "What are you doing, you brute? Put me down."

"You'd have to let go of my neck first." He grinned and leaned down to kiss her.

Another male voice came from the door. "Yes, Eloise. You'll have to let go of his neck first."

They turned to look at the intruder. "Ross," she gasped. Then silence. Deafening silence.

CHAPTER 8

"*W*hat are you doing here?" she finally spat out.

"What are *you* doing here?" His usual complacency gone, Ross curled his hands into fists, a rare display of jealousy. "Put my girlfriend *down*."

"The girlfriend you haven't bothered to contact for over six months? Sorry, buddy. Last time I checked, a fella doesn't carry a torch for a girl and not call or write." Victor set Eloise on the floor, and she stepped between the two men.

"Ross, this is Victor... He's the postman for Ridgecrest." She immediately realized her mistake when she saw the hurt in Vic's eyes at her introduction and made an attempt to soothe his ego. "Victor, this is Ross, my friend from LA."

Oh, god, that didn't help. What am I doing? Postman? Friend? She wanted to start over. No, she wanted to join Punkinhead under the couch.

"Friend? Friend?" Ross took a step forward, pointing a finger at her face. "I've sent you money, *kept* you, *gave* you a place to stay, and I'm a *friend?*" He poked her chest with each emphasized word.

"Back off." Victor's words were low, but his face held

barely contained anger, his dark eyes flashing and dangerous. "If you touch her again, you will regret it."

"Don't threaten me in my own house. And for the record, I did send a letter and said I was on my way home. Now I know why you weren't back in Los Angeles." Ignoring the threat, he poked at Eloise's chest again. "Why, you little floozy—"

Bam!

Ross landed in a corner, a look of shock on his face as he rubbed his jaw.

Elli rushed over to Ross. "Are you okay? Oh, Victor, how could you?"

"Don't touch her again." He stretched his fingers out and then fisted his hand again.

"Victor, I think you should leave."

"*I* should leave?"

Ross stood up slowly, shook his head one way, then the other. He put both hands up in the air. "Hey, now, take it easy. A man leaves to make a name for himself, comes back to propose to his best girl—of course, he'd be a little upset to see her in the arms of another guy."

"Propose?" Eloise couldn't breathe. "Is this a line?" Her thoughts became jumbled, and she couldn't think. *Now? Now he wants to get married?*

"C'mon, doll." His hands spread out in a pleading motion. "Would I kid about something like marriage? Tell this schmuck to go, and I'll explain everything."

She turned to the man who had rescued her more times than Superman saved Lois. A fight would not help this situation, and Ross had a right to a private conversation. But it wouldn't be easy to convince Victor to leave.

"Yes, I think you should go for now. This is *his* house." The hurt in those coffee eyes made her wish she could take those words back.

"Tell me you aren't considering his proposal?"

"Look, we need some time alone and—"

"Tell me you are not considering his proposal. Hollywood might listen to his spiel, but Elli would kick him out on his ear."

His words pinched her heart, but she and Ross owed one another an explanation.

"Ross deserves—"

"So you are." He swiped a hand over his face, as if trying to make sense of it all. "At least I found out before it was too late. I must admit, though, you sure had me fooled." He turned to the man he'd just knocked to the floor. "She's all yours, wise guy. You'll make a great team. She's quite an actress."

He walked out the door without a backward glance. There had been such finality in his voice. A pain twisted in her gut, and tears sprang to her eyes. Her hand reached out after him, and she tried to call his name, but no sound came out. Ross put an arm around her shoulder and squeezed, his usual charm and self-assurance back in place.

"I'm sorry about that scene. Poor yokel, I can tell he's stuck on you. Who could blame him?"

His words sounded muffled and far off. Flashbacks of Victor ran through her mind. That first day with Punkin, the diner, meeting his mother. It had all been so wonderful. *He* had been so wonderful, and she'd never been happier. Eloise saw him in the sandstorm, risking his life for her, remembered his kiss and his gentle touch. A tiny voice screamed in her head. *I went too far. I've ruined everything.*

A tear slid down her cheek. Chase your dream and have no regrets. *I'm sorry, Mama.*

"Well, what do you say, doll? Let's get hitched."

* * *

THE HIGH SCHOOL gym was packed. The whole town—well, almost the whole town—had turned out for the annual party. Victor didn't know which was worse. Staying home so everyone would know something went wrong or coming here and pretending everything was fine. Valentine's Day wasn't the time you told people you'd lost the love of your life.

A pair of black-strapped heels entered his line of vision. "What the heck is going on?" Rita demanded in her subtle way.

"Nothing. Everything is fine," he answered without looking up. "Just peach pie and blue sky."

"Oh, applesauce!" She pushed at his shoulder. "Where's your girl?"

He shrugged his shoulders. Now a pair of scuffed but polished dress shoes joined the black straps. "What's his problem?" asked Tiny.

"Woman trouble," Rita answered for him.

"Did she go back to L.A.?" A low whistle. "That surprises me. I thought she was settling in right nice."

"That makes two of us," he agreed, giving up the pretense. "Her Hollywood Man came back and proposed."

Rita's hands flew to her hips. "Did she know about your ring?"

"Hadn't asked her yet. Besides, it doesn't matter. If she prefers the city boy, I don't want her anyway."

"Horsefeathers!" Tiny waved a finger at him. "You didn't even try to persuade her. How do you know who she'd choose?"

"That's the point, isn't it? If there's a choice, then she doesn't love me."

Tiny rolled his eyes. "You're a smart man, Burnham, but you don't have a clue about women. Mary! Mary, come quick."

Mary waved from across the room, her red satin skirt glimmering in the dim light. "Coming."

"I'm going to tell you a story."

A groan escaped him. Victor didn't want to be rude, but he wasn't in the mood for a story of happy ever after. Not tonight. Coming here had been a mistake.

Mary joined the group, and it started again. "Oh, Vic, you look so sad. What's—"

"The movie guy proposed to Hollywood."

"No! But you showed her the ring?"

Patience. These are my friends, and they will be here long after Elli is gone.

Rita took over. "He didn't tell her. Just walked away."

"Oh dear." She made a *tsk, tsk* sound. "I never took you for a dope."

"Look—" Victor's hands went up in self-defense. "I don't really want a lesson in love tonight. I thank you all for your concern, but it's time for me to go."

"It's the kiss that did it for me," Mary said with a nod.

"How many proposals did you have that summer?" Tiny asked, elbowing Victor. "A dozen?"

She giggled. "Goodness, no. Three for sure, though." She put her hand through her husband's arm and tapped her chin. "Yes, three. Tiny was fit to be tied. It was such fun."

"Fun? You enjoyed ripping a man's heart out?" He was beginning to think he didn't know these people.

"I did no such thing. But Dan Panker had me wondering. I thought of what he could give me and had stars in my eyes for a while." She shook her head. "Then Tiny came over, boiling mad. I told him I wouldn't marry him if he were the last man on earth."

Victor waited.

"Then he kissed me. He kissed me and said, 'Can Dan do that to you?' It hit me." She leaned over and kissed Tiny on the cheek. "That warmth only one person in the world can create in your soul is worth more than a fine house and pretty clothes. That warmth will last through the years and keep the chill from your bones when you're old and gray."

"You'll be just as beautiful when you're old and gray, sweetheart."

"See, I told you he had finesse."

Victor put his hands in his pockets, wondering how to escape this attack. Mary's story was sweet, but it was too late. He had already made his stand and opened the door for Hollywood Man. If his foot would reach, he'd kick himself.

"Well, you think about it," Rita said. "You didn't throw the ring in China Lake did you?"

"No, it cost me a month's wages." Not that it mattered. A year's wages would have been worth it. The couples dancing depressed him. His perfect night had turned into a nightmare. The door was clear, so he made his exit.

At the top of the stairs, the chilled air hit him, and he slid his hands in his pockets. There it was—the box that held his broken dreams. Stepping out of the light, he leaned against the stone wall and closed his eyes. He shouldn't have left it the way he did. They should have at least had a real goodbye, had some closure. *Elli, Elli. How will I ever be able to love someone else?*

"Victor?"

Eyes still closed, he wondered if her voice came from inside his head.

"Victor, could we talk?" *Be careful what you wish for.*

"Where's Hollywood Man?"

"Filling up his car. He wanted you to know he doesn't have any hard feelings. The house goes up for sale next week."

"*Hmph.* Good to know."

The band began again. Strains of Louis Armstrong's "A Kiss to Build a Dream On" floated through the double doors.

"I never meant to hurt you. Ross caught me by surprise, that's all."

The lead singer's bluesy voice wafted around their heads.

Give me a kiss...

"To build a dream on," Elli sang softly.

Victor opened his eyes. She stood there in a navy swing coat that made her light-blue eyes sparkle. If this was it, he wanted something to remember.

Sweetheart, I ask no more than this...

"Dance with me." He held out his arms, and she stepped into them.

"A kiss to build a dream on," he whispered in her ear.

They needed a proper goodbye, he thought as she laid her head on his shoulder, and they swayed to the music.

Give me your lips for just a moment...

Leaning his cheek against her hair, he breathed in the scent of her one last time, memorizing the curve of her body, how her hand fit into his.

And my imagination...

. . .

"WILL MAKE THAT MOMENT LIVE," Victor crooned as they swayed, body to body.

He pulled back ever so slightly to see her face, trace the smoothness of her cheeks, the hollow in her neck. But he only saw the tears shining in her eyes, the red lips parted, the regret...

She sang along with the band, "Leave me one thing before—"

Victor captured her words with his mouth before she could finish. Her lips were velvet, her tongue like honey. He wanted to close his eyes and never stop kissing her. Her curves fit against him as if made specifically for him. Desire surged through him, wanting to mark her, claim her, put another fist into Hollywood Man's face. But most of all, he wanted Elli to be happy.

A kiss to build a dream on...

He tasted her again, a man hungry for a final memory, and she clung to him as if wanting the same. Her hands moved to his face and traced the long lines in his cheeks. Their tongues danced; their rhythm never faltered. The song ended, yet they continued to move, a sensual circle in the shadows of the building. The world had faded into the background, leaving only the two of them suspended in this precious moment.

The band announced a swing contest, and Elli's hands trailed down his chest. "Victor, I..."

"You better go, or you'll miss your ride back to LA."

"I'm not going back," she said in a weak voice. "Even if you won't have me, I'm not going back."

He grabbed her by the shoulders and gave her a rough shake. "Don't play with me. You made your choice."

A sob escaped her, and she nodded. "Yes, I did. And I chose you. Of course I chose you."

"You chose me?" He pulled her to him and held her in a fierce hug. "Why didn't you say so? Do you have any idea what you put me through?"

She nodded and sniffed, trying to swipe at her nose. "Me too. I'm so sorry. I'm so so sorry."

"Are you sure?"

Another nod.

Swallow your pride. It won't keep you warm at night. Wise words from his father years ago. He wouldn't let her get away again. This was it.

Victor fumbled in his pocket and found the box. He went down on one knee, opened the box, and raised his eyes to hers. The tears spilled over her lashes. "Will you marry me, Eloise Kolby?"

She took a shaky breath, her hand on her mouth and squeaked out, "Yes."

He stood up and, lifting her hand, gently placed the ring on her finger. Her arms went around his neck, laughing and crying.

"Yes, Victor Burnham, I'll marry you. Yes."

The small crowd, waiting just inside the entrance, let out a cheer. Mary said to Rita, "I told him it was the kiss."

EPILOGUE

June 1952
Chicago, Illinois

*E*lli woke, then blinked. Unfamiliar wallpaper confronted her on the opposite wall, and a satin bedspread was pulled up to her neck. She heard the water running in the ensuite bathroom and smiled. She was Mrs. Victor Burnham. And they were at the Palmer House Hotel in Chicago. The Palmer House!

Victor had asked her a hundred and one questions about her birthplace while they decided where to go for their honeymoon. She'd included this hotel as one of the ritziest places in the city, describing the Tiffany Peacock door of gilded bronze just inside the entrance and the Grecian frescoes on the two-story lobby ceiling. He'd remembered and surprised her with a room.

"It's my first day in Chicago," Vic called from behind the

closed door. "Better get up and get moving. Your family is expecting us."

She grinned. "Technically, it's your second day."

He opened the door and popped his head out, shaving cream still on one side of his face. "Technically, I've only had one night in the Windy City," he said, waggling his eyebrows.

Elli giggled, embarrassed as she thought of their intimate evening, and threw a pillow at him. She dressed in a simple pale-blue halter dress, tossed her sunglasses in her purse, and slipped on her white flats. She ran a comb through her hair and clipped on a pair of gold earrings. The diamond on her left hand, sitting smartly atop her gold wedding band, seemed to wink at her. Mrs. Burnham.

The wedding had been short and sweet in front of the Justice of the Peace. Elli and Vic had laughed as they ran down the courthouse steps, dodging the cascade of rice. It seemed the entire town of Ridgecrest had come to wish them well and see them off on their honeymoon. Victor's mother had cried, complained of ruining her makeup, then hugged them both, wishing them all the happiness she'd had in her marriage.

Now, as the newlyweds finished breakfast, her stomach began to knot. It had been so long since she'd seen her siblings. Her sister Kay, a faithful correspondent, had been the one to write and inform her of their father's passing. Allen, now fourteen, and Jimmy, twelve, were growing fast. Elli barely knew her stepmother, Ruth, but Kay had grown very close to her. Throughout Eloise's time in California, she had read Kay's letters of the strengthening bond between her father's second wife and the children.

It turned out Ruth had considered herself a spinster. When Mr. Kirby had suggested a marriage of convenience, the woman had jumped at the chance to have a family. She had slowly gained the children's trust and become an ally.

Elli's father hadn't known Ruth had her own money. And she wasn't stingy when it came to "her family." Still, Eloise was nervous about this reunion.

"Penny for your thoughts," said Victor as they drove along Lake Shore Drive. The crashing waves sparkled in the morning sun. The breeze ruffled beneath her scarf, and she breathed in the smells of the city.

"I'm thinking what a lucky girl I am to have such a handsome and thoughtful husband." She grinned at him. "Are you sure you're ready to meet my family?"

"Not all of them, right?"

She shook her head. "No, just the younger ones."

"And Ruth." He gave her a side-glance. "Still feeling guilty about how you left?"

Elli blinked back hot tears and nodded. "And she turned out to be a wonderful stepmother."

"No evil mirrors or poisoned apples?" He gave her a wink.

They parked in front of the old brownstone, and she grabbed the gym bag with their swimming suits. They walked up two flights of stairs. Pausing in front of the door, memories rushed her, and she took a deep breath. Victor put his arm around her waist and gave her a squeeze. "I'm here, sweetheart."

She gave him a grateful smile and knocked on the door. An older woman with dark hair and only a few gray hairs answered. Her smile was immediate and warm, reaching her hazel eyes. She opened the door wider and ushered them into the living room.

"Kay," she called. "They're here." Ruth turned to Eloise and gave her a hug. She smelled of lavender and cinnamon rolls.

Allen sauntered in, his dark hair slicked back and a crooked smile on his handsome face. Jimmy was right on his heels, imitating his brother's walk and smoothing back his blond waves framing his still boyish, round face. Both brothers stood in front of her, eyes everywhere except on their sister, hands deep in their dungaree pockets.

Elli's heart chased away her remaining trepidation and threw her arms around both boys. "You've grown so! Allen, you're a young man already. Jimmy, you're so tall." She blinked back the tears that once again threatened.

Both boys awkwardly returned the hug, patting Elli's back. "You're prettier," mumbled Allen.

Then Kay whooshed in, and the girls were hugging and rocking and crying. Victor handed Elli his handkerchief, and she blew her nose, sending the boys into a round of guffaws.

"When did you dye your hair?" she asked Kay, noting her sister's once auburn waves were now a burnished blonde, just touching her shoulders.

"After she saw Grace Kelly in High Noon," spouted Jimmy.

"Hush, you little heathen," Kay muttered, turning to Victor. "Mr. Burnham?"

"I prefer Victor," he said with a nod, holding out his hand and shaking each family member as they were formally introduced.

"Would you like some coffee?" asked Ruth, heading toward the kitchen.

"Not for me," said Victor.

"I had too much at breakfast," added Elli, giving Ruth her warmest smile. "We thought we'd all take a walk along the lake this afternoon. After we catch up, of course." Her step-mother's smile was equally heartfelt, so Elli knew she was pleased at being included in the invitation.

Victor sat on the couch, his long legs bent at the knee, a grin curving his lips. The brothers flanked him, plopping down one on each side. Elli laughed when Jimmy patted the couch beside him. "There's still room, Elli."

When Victor mentioned baseball, she knew her husband had charmed the boys. "Did you know we have there's an LA Wrigley Field?" he asked. "The Angels aren't major league, of course, but they play great baseball and have sent some great talent to Chicago. Do you like the Cubs?"

"Like crazy," said Allen. "The Angels are the Cubs' farm team."

"I'd love to see a game at Chicago's Wrigley Field. But Elli's a girl and they don't—"

"We'll go," yelled Jimmy, flying off the couch like a pogo stick. "Who would want to see a game with a girl?"

"They're playing their fourth game against Pittsburgh on Thursday. Cubbies 2, Pirates 1. We gotta win, or we'll be tied," Allen said, his tone serious. "Do you think we can get tickets?"

"Oh, I bet we can if we aren't too picky about the seats." Victor bent his head and covered one side of his mouth, as if sharing a secret with Allen.

"A seat's a seat," Allen said knowingly.

"But what'll we do with—" Jimmy jerked his head toward Elli.

"Couldn't they go shopping or do their hair or something?" asked Allen.

"I thought Ruth, Kay, and I would have lunch at the Palmer House that day, then maybe some shopping on State Street?" Elli turned to the ladies. She and Victor had discussed this on their way to Chicago. "Victor could drop you off at the hotel when he picks the boys up for the game."

"But it's your honeymoon," cried Kay. "You don't want to spend it with us."

"I want to spend time with my family. And I'm in desperate need of some girl talk," confided Elli. "We'll have plenty of time for romance this week."

The three women sat on blankets at Foster Beach,

watching the "boys." Victor was explaining the basics of surf-boarding, without the board. His arms rose and fell, one imitating the waves, the other was the surfer. The brothers' heads followed every movement.

Elli had just finished telling them how she and Victor had met.

"Fate," Kay said with a sigh. "He met you in the diner, and you were destined to be together one day."

"He loves children," commented Ruth. "He'll make a good father."

"Yes, he will." Eloise blushed, then grabbed her sister's hand. "Would you like to visit California? Victor thinks we could manage the plane tickets if—"

"I'm happy to buy them," interrupted Ruth.

"But it would cost—"

Ruth shook her head. "At forty-five, I inherited a large sum from my grandmother before I met your father. I was at an age where, if a man knew about the money, he would pay attention to me for the wrong reasons. When your father offered to 'save me from spinsterhood' by marrying me, I saw my only chance at having a family." She reached over and lovingly tucked a lock of Kay's hair behind her ear. "I admit I never loved your father, but I am devoted to his children."

Elli drew in a deep breath and closed her eyes. Her mother would have liked Ruth. They might have been friends. "I'm sorry I didn't give you a chance."

Ruth smiled and squeezed Elli's hand. "You were searching for your future. It was what your mother wanted for you. And she was right." Her stepmother's gaze turned to Victor and the boys. "You found love and happiness in California. I imagine she's smiling down on all of us right now."

Without thinking, Elli threw her arms around Ruth. "I think you're right. Thank you."

After an afternoon of sun and swimming, Victor tried to buy them all hot dogs at the food stand on the beach. The boys rejected the idea, explaining their brother-in-law needed to try a true Chicago hot dog.

"Ya gotta go to Tony's Pump Room, Vic," said Allen, now feeling quite at home with his new brother-in-law. "There's nothing better on this earth."

"Well, then. A Chicago dog it is. And how much will this wiener in a bun set me back? Should we change into something fancier for the Pump Room?"

The boys laughed, grabbing their stomachs and shaking their heads. "It's just a hot dog stand."

Elli slipped her hand into the crook of Victor's elbow. "We may have to drive around a bit to find him. He changes corners every so often."

The famous Tony's white cart with red wheels was finally located on Addison and Lake Shore. As the group gathered around the large cart fashioned like an old mini stagecoach, Elli placed an order for six dogs with "everything on" and six Cokes. Tony, an Italian immigrant from Sicily, greeted them with a smile and made a show of creating Victor's first Chicago-style hot dog. "You're in for a treat, my friend."

"I've never seen so many toppings on a wiener," said Victor, watching Tony at work.

The city staple began with a poppyseed bun and a steaming Vienna all-beef hot dog. Then came the condiments: with chopped onions, a tomato slice, a dill pickle spear, glow in the dark pickle relish, sport peppers, mustard, and the mandatory celery salt.

"I never would have combined these ingredients together in one bun," Victor said around his second bite. "This is…" He closed his eyes. "Boss, baby, boss."

Allen and Jimmy looked at each and busted out laughing.

***

End of the week

Victor took a last look at Lake Michigan as they left Chicago. The traffic was much like LA. He'd been surprised at how much the lake looked like the ocean. The buildings were older, some taller, some dingier. But there was a different kind of excitement in the crowded streets, more of a purpose, a rush to get somewhere. He'd enjoyed his visit but preferred his little desert town.

Their honeymoon had been a week of adventure and love, for both the new couple and Elli's family. Victor had thoroughly enjoyed his new brothers-in-law. Kay had promised to write to the other siblings and see if they could all get together over Thanksgiving. He cast a side-glance at Elli. She positively glowed as they headed back to California.

"Are you sure you don't mind all of them visiting us in Ridgecrest?" Elli was snuggled next to him, her head resting on his shoulder.

"It was good of you to invite Ruth too." Victor kissed the top of her scarf that held down her blond curls, the wind whipping through the open windows.

"I like her. She makes my brothers and sisters happy, treats them like her own. And she doesn't hold a grudge."

"I think my mother will like her. If it's too crowded on Ivy Lane, Ruth might want to stay with Mom." Victor's heart was full. There was nothing like family, and he'd instinctively known Elli would never have been fully happy without reconnecting to hers and making peace with her stepmother. His thoughts strayed to his hometown.

He missed the old house. Victor had always known 19 Ivy Lane would be part of his destiny. The property had beckoned him with a solid foundation for a promising future.

Now it was time to start filling those empty rooms with their own family. The place seemed to beg for laughter and children. He put his arm around Elli and drew in a deep breath. He had waited a long time to begin his life there.

Patience is a virtue, his mother had told him as a boy.

Patience had certainly reaped great rewards for him and Elli.

"Let's go home, Hollywood," he said, laughing when Elli smacked his chest good-naturedly at the use of her old nickname. "A new show is about to begin, and this time, we're the stars."

REVIEWS ARE a writer's life blood. If you enjoyed this story, please consider leaving a few words at your favorite retailer.

https://books2read.com/19-ivy-lane

ABOUT THE AUTHOR

USA TODAY best-selling author Aubrey Wynne was an elementary teacher by trade, champion of children and animals by conscience, and author by night. She resides in the Midwest with her husband, dogs, horses, mule, and barn cats. Obsessions include wine, history, travel, trail riding, and all things Christmas. Her *Charming in Chicago* series has received the Golden Quill, Aspen Gold, Heart of Excellence, and the Gayle Wilson Award of Excellence and twice nominated as a Rone finalist by InD'tale Magazine.

Aubrey's first love is historical romance. She has two series, *Once Upon a Widow* (Sweet Regency) and *Paddy's Peelers* (historical mystery).

Find Aubrey:

Website: http://www.aubreywynne.com/

Facebook: http://facebook.com/magnificentvalor

 Twitter: http://twitter.com/aubreywynne51

Instagram: http://instagram.com/Aubreywynne51

Bookbub: https://www.bookbub.com/profile/aubrey-wynne

Goodreads: https://www.goodreads.com/author/show/7383937.Aubrey_Wynne

Facebook Reading Group: https://www.facebook.com/groups/AubreyWynnesEverAfters/

Subscribe to Aubrey's newsletter for new releases, exclusive excerpts, and free stories:

Newsletter: http://www.subscribepage.com/k3f1z5

Dante's Gift - Kathleen James looked forward to an intimate dinner and an engagement ring. Dominic Lawrence planned this marriage proposal for six months. Nothing can go wrong—until his Nonna calls.

Can Antonia's romantic WWII tale of an American GI and a very special collie bring these two hearts together at Christmas?

Merry Christmas, Henry – Henry, a shy and talented artist, moonlights as a security guard at a museum and loses his heart to a beautiful, melancholy woman in a painting. As his obsession grows, he finds a kindred soul who helps him in his search for happiness. On Christmas Eve, Henry dares to take a chance on love and fulfill his dream.

Pete's Mighty Purty Privies – Pete McNutt needs customers for his new business. Spring has arrived and it's prime time Privy Season. After much consideration, he refines his sales pitch and heads to the monthly meeting of the Women's Library Association.

To Cast a Cliché - The evil Queen Lucinda exacts revenge on a royal poet by casting a spell of never-ending clichés upon the kingdom. Will the clever King Richard thwart his step-mother's magic and save the good people of Maxim? Test your literary knowledge and enjoy an entertaining spoof on fairytales.

Rolf's Quest – Time is running out for the royal wizard of Henry II. Rolf's quest: find genuine love and lift the enchantment that has imprisoned his ancestor, Merlin, for centuries. Now he must win Melissa's heart without the use of magic. She desires him, but will she defy her family and refuse her betrothed? Or will Rolf be doomed to a life of bitterness like his ancestors before him?

ALSO BY AUBREY WYNNE

Other Contemporary Romance by Aubrey Wynne

Charming in Chicago series

Merry Christmas, Henry (Charming in Chicago #1)

Preditors and Editors Readers' Choice, N.N. Light Best Short Story Award

"Captivating Christmas Choice!"

K--dle Book Review

"Short, sweet, and stunning!"

Great Reads

Henry, a shy and talented artist, moonlights as a security guard at a museum and loses his heart to a beautiful, melancholy woman in a painting. As his obsession grows, he finds a kindred soul who helps him in his search for happiness. On Christmas Eve, Henry dares to take a chance on love and fulfill his dream.

Dante's Gift (Charming in Chicago #2)

Winner of the RWA Golden Quill, Aspen Gold, and Heart of Excellence

Rone finalist, InD'tale Magazine

"Wynne has crafted a beautiful short story guaranteed to warm your heart and make you sigh."

"... a wonderfully poignant holiday romantic tale that intertwines two love stories..."

Jersey Girls Book Reviews

"A lovely sweet romance!"

Book Addicts

Kathleen James has put her practical side away for once and looks forward to the perfect romantic evening: an intimate dinner with the man of her dreams—and an engagement ring. She is not prepared to hear that he wants to bring his grandmother back from Italy to live with him.

Dominic Lawrence has planned this marriage proposal for six months. Nothing can go wrong— until his Nonna calls. Now he must interrupt the tenderest night of Katie's life with the news that another woman will be under their roof.

When Antonia's sister dies, she finds herself longing to be back in the states. An Italian wartime bride from the '40s, she knows how precious love can be. Can her own story of an American soldier and a very special collie once again bring two hearts together at Christmas?

Paper Love (Charming in Chicago #3)

Bragg Medallion recipient, Winner of Gayle Wilson Award for Excellence

Recommended by InD'Tale magazine

"This author has a knack for love stories that make your heart flutter."

Reads2Love Book Reviews

"Aubrey Wynne is a talented author weaving a descriptive setting, cultural details, historical facts, and inspirational romance into a delightful read."

Growing up in a Papua New Guinea mission, Joss Palmateer is a gentle soul with a unique view of life. Still adjusting to a new home in the U.S. and the sudden loss of her mother, love is the last thing on her mind.

Sexy physical therapist, Ben Montgomery, meets his sister's friend and the sparks fly. He takes it as a silent challenge when she ignores his advances, but it's her extraordinary inner beauty that captures his heart.

With the help of a stray homing pigeon and an old origami legend, Ben sets an unwavering course of romance to win her love.

For the Love of Laura Beth (Charming in Chicago #4)

Rone Finalist, InD'tale Magazine

Finalist for Best Book Buyers, The Maggie, and The Beverly awards

"Beautifully written and tells a story that will allow readers to experience the turmoil that war can bring to the lives of those who must endure its heartbreak."

"This isn't your typical boy-meets-girl-they-get-married-and-live-happily-ever-after-the-end story. This is sweet romance in the midst of real life hardships and pain, and a love that will press through and triumph."

The Korean War destroyed their plans, but the battle at home may shatter their hearts...

Laura Beth Walters fell in love with Joe McCall when she was six years old. Now she is counting the days until Joey graduates from college so they can marry and begin their life together. But the Korean War rips their neatly laid plans to shreds. Instead of a college fraternity, Joey joins a platoon. Laura Beth trades a traditional wedding for a quick trip to the courthouse.

The couple endure the hardship of separation, but the true battle is faced when Joey returns from the war. Their marriage is soon tested beyond endurance. Laura must find a way to accept the tragedy thrown in their path or lose the love that has kept them anchored for so long. With a determination that only comes from the heart, Joe relentlessly fights an invisible enemy... for the love of Laura Beth.

19 Ivy Lane (Charming in Chicago #5)

Eloise Kolby leaves her hometown of Chicago and arrives in 1950s Hollywood with dreams of becoming a movie star. While waiting for her big break, she falls for charming script-writer Ross Wilson. But when Ross promises her a big surprise, it's not a ring, but a new project on location in Italy—for him alone. Putting her dreams on hold, she agrees to investigate a house he inherited in a small desert town outside LA.

Ridgecrest Postman Victor Burnham has always wanted to buy the property on Ivy Lane. But from the moment the beautiful, mysterious blonde moves into "his" house, his life becomes complicated. Their daily rendezvous at the mailbox has tongues wagging and Victor longing to share his dream house.

When Eloise's long-awaited letter arrives, signaling Ross's return, she must choose—her new life on Ivy Lane with a steadfast postman and the promise of a family or the allure of fame and Hollywood glamour. Whose heart will be stamped Return to Sender?

Small Town Romance Standalone

Saving Grace (A Small Town Romance)

Finalist for the Maggie and Holt awards

"This unique piece has the reader traveling between the early 1700s and the early 2000s with ease and amazement. The audience truly feels sorrow for Grace and Chloe and is able to connect with each woman for the hardships they are overcoming. The attention to historical facts and details leave one breathless especially upon learning the people from the past did exist, and the memorial erected still stands."

InD'Tale Magazine

A tortured soul meets a shattered heart...

Chloe Hicks' life consisted of an egocentric ex-husband, a pile of bills, and an equine business in foreclosure until a fire destroys the stable and her beloved ranch horse. What little hope she has left is smashed after the marshal suspects arson. She escapes the accusing eyes of her hometown, but not the memories and melancholy.

Jackson Hahn, Virginia Beach's local historian, has his eyes on the mysterious new woman in town. When she enters his office, he is struck by her haunting beauty and the raw pain in her eyes. Her descriptions of the odd events happening in her bungalow pique his curiosity.

The sexy historian distracts Chloe with the legend of a woman wrongly accused of witchcraft. She is drawn to the story and the similarities of events that plagued their lives. Perhaps the past can help heal the present. But danger lurks in the shadows...

Historical Romance

Once Upon a Widow series (sweet Regency)

Paddy's Peelers series (historical mystery)